Sugar and Spice

D0587232

Sugar and Spice

JEAN URE

Illustrated by Karen Donnelly

HarperCollins *Children's Books*

for Mariam

First published in Great Britain by HarperCollins *Children's Books* in 2005
HarperCollins *Children's Books* is a division of HarperCollins*Publishers* Ltd,
77-85 Fulham Palace Road, Hammersmith, London W6 8JB

The HarperCollins *Children's Books* website address is
www.harpercollinschildrensbooks.co.uk

1

Text © Jean Ure 2005
Illustrations © Karen Donnelly 2005

The author and illustrator assert the moral right to be
identified as the author and illustrator of this work.

ISBN 0 00 716137 9

Printed and bound in England by
Clays Ltd, St Ives plc

one

"Ruth! Time to get up."

Time to get up. Get yourself dressed. I'm not telling you again! Every morning, same old thing.

"Did you hear me? Ruth?"

Yes, I did! I heard you.

"I'd like some kind of response, please!"

And then she'll go, *I hope you haven't gone back to sleep?*

"I hope you haven't gone back to sleep?"

Get up, get dressed. How many more times?

Why doesn't she just give it a rest?

"Do I have to shout myself hoarse? Get yourself up this instant!" Mum suddenly appeared like a tornado at the bedroom door. "And get your sisters up, as well. For goodness' sake! It's gone seven o'clock."

Boo hoo! So what?

"Do you want to be late for school? Because you will be!"

Don't care if I am. Sooner be late than get there early.

"All this big talk," said Mum. "Going to be a *doctor*. Going to pass *exams*. You'll be lucky to get a job in Tesco's if you don't shift yourself and make a bit of an effort!"

Mum had no idea. She didn't know what it was like. She didn't know how much I hated it. Hated, hated, HATED it!

"Ruth, I'm warning you." Mum marched across to the window and yanked back the curtains. I could tell she was in a mood. "I can't take much more of this! I'm running out of patience."

So why couldn't she just go away and leave me alone? I burrowed further down the bed, wrapping myself up in the duvet. I was safe in the duvet. In bed, in the bedroom. At home. I'd have liked to stay there for always. Never go out again anywhere, ever. And specially not to *school*.

"I mean it," said Mum. "I can't be doing with this battle every morning. I've got your dad to see to, I've got your brother to see to... now, come along! Shift yourself! I don't have all day." And with one tug she hauled the duvet right off me.

"*Mu-u-um!*" I squealed in protest, curling myself up into a tight little ball and clinging to the pillow with both hands. "Mum, *please!*"

"Enough," said Mum. "Just get yourself up. And don't forget your sisters!"

They were still asleep. They'd sleep through an earthquake, those two. All snuggled up together, Kez

with her thumb in her mouth, Lisa on her back, blowing bubbles. Ah! Bless. Like a pair of little angels. *I don't think*. Actually, I suppose, they're not too bad, as sisters go.

They can sometimes be quite sweet, like when Kez climbs on to your lap for a cuddle, or Lisa does her show-off dancing, very solemn, with her fingers splayed out and her face all scrunched up with the effort she's putting into it. She's really cute when she does her dancing! Other times, though, they can be a total pain. This is because Mum lets them get away with just about everything. Dad too. He's even worse! *Spare the rod and spoil the child* is what one of my nans says. I know you're not allowed to beat your children these days (Nan was beaten with a *cane* when she was young) but I do think Mum and Dad ought to exercise a little bit more discipline. I try to, but it's a losing battle. They just cheek me or go running off to Dad.

"Dad! Ruth's being mean!"

Then I'm the one who gets the blame, cos I'm twelve years old and they're only little, except I don't personally think nine is as little as all that. I'm sure I wouldn't have been rude to my older sister when I was nine. If I'd had an older sister. I certainly wouldn't have helped myself to her things without asking, which is what Lisa is always doing and which drives me completely *nuts*. Kezzy is only six, so maybe there is a bit of an excuse for her. Maybe.

Anyway, I wasn't wasting my breath pleading with them. I just got hold of the pillows and yanked. That got their attention! Kez blinked at me like a baby owl. Lisa started wailing.

"Get up!" I said, and kicked the bed. Unlike Mum, I don't stand for any nonsense. You have to be firm. "Go on! Get up!"

"Don't want to get up," grumbled Lisa. "Haven't finished sleeping."

"Can't help that," I said. "You have to go to school." When I was nine, I loved going to school. I couldn't get there fast enough. "Who've you got this term?" I said.

Lisa sniffed and said, "Mrs Henson."

I felt this great well of envy. Lisa didn't know how

lucky she was! Mrs Henson was just the best teacher I ever had. *The best.* When I told Mrs Henson I wanted to be a doctor she didn't laugh or say that I'd better not set my sights too high. She said, "Well, and why not? I'm sure that would be possible, if you work hard enough." She made you feel like you could do anything you wanted. You could be a doctor or a teacher. You could even be Prime Minister!

"Mrs Henson is just so lovely," I said.

Lisa said she wasn't lovely. "She tells me off."

"In that case, you're obviously doing something wrong," I said.

"I'm not doing anything wrong. She just picks on me!"

"Mrs Henson doesn't *pick* on people," I said. I felt quite cross with my stupid little sister. Fancy having a wonderful teacher like Mrs Henson and not appreciating her! If I still had Mrs Henson, Mum wouldn't have to bawl and bellow at me every morning. I'd be out of bed like a shot! "You just get dressed," I said. "And stop whining!"

I dragged on my school clothes, which I hated almost as much as I hated school. *Black skirt, grey jumper.* Ugh! It made me feel miserable before I even got there. I'd always looked forward to having a school uniform as I thought it would be something to be, like, proud of, but nobody could be proud of going to

Parkfield High. (Or Krapfilled High, as some of the boys called it. I know it sounds rather rude, but I think it's more suited than Parkfield since there isn't any park and there isn't any field and it's absolutely *crud*. Which is why I hated it.)

Lisa was now complaining that she couldn't find her knickers and Kez had gone and put her top on inside out, so I had to stop and grovel on the floor, all covered in shoes and socks and toys and books and dirty spoons

and empty pots. I found the missing knickers, which Lisa then screamed she couldn't wear on account of someone having gone and trodden on them and left a muddy footprint; so we had a bit of an argument about that, with me telling her that no one was going to see them, and her saying that they might, and me saying how? – I mean, *how*? "Boys peek when you go upstairs," she said, which meant in the end we had to get out a clean pair, by which time Kez had not only got her top on inside out but had put both feet down the same leg of her trousers and couldn't work out what to do about it. Honestly! My sisters! Was it any wonder I was always late for school? Not that I cared. Nobody ever noticed, anyway.

In the kitchen, Mum was putting on her make-up, filling lunch boxes, getting breakfast, dressing Sammy. Sammy is my little brother. He's four years old and is even more spoilt than Kez and Lisa. This is because he's a *boy*. There is a lot of sexism going on in my family.

Mum said, "Ah, Ruth! There you are. About time! Just keep an eye on the toast for me, love. Oh, and lay the table, will you, there's a good girl."

So I kept an eye on the toast and laid the table and finished dressing Sammy and removed the raw carrot from my lunch box as I'm *not a rabbit*, whatever Mum may think, and put some more peanut butter in my sandwiches when she wasn't looking, and got out the Sugar Puffs, and got out the milk, and finally took Dad's breakfast tray in to him, being careful not to spill his mug of tea. Dad always has his breakfast in bed, then Mum helps him get up and settles him comfortably for the day before rushing off to work, dropping Sammy off at Reception and Kez and Lisa at Juniors. I have to make my own way, by bus, but that's all right; I'm quite good at getting around London. It's easy when you know how. Also it means that I can d-a-w-d-l-e and not get into school too early. If there is any danger of getting in too early I wander round the back streets until I can be sure that the first bell will have gone.

It's quite scary in the playground, even in the girls' part, as there are all these different gangs that have their special areas where you're not allowed to go. Unless, of course, you happen to belong to them. I do not belong to any of them, so I have to be really careful where I tread. It's like picking your way through a minefield. Any minute you can stray into someone else's territory, and then it's like, "Where d'you think you're going?"

I don't know why I never belonged to a gang. Cos nobody ever asked me, I guess. When we were at Juniors we all mixed together. My best friend was Millie and my second best friend was Mariam. I thought that when we went to senior school we'd all go on being friends. But almost the minute we arrived at Parkfield, they got swallowed up into gangs. The gangs were, like, really exclusive – *if you're not one of us, we don't want to know you*. It meant that when we were at school, all the people I'd been juniors with almost didn't talk to me any more. There was a gang of white girls I could have joined, maybe, if I'd wanted, but there was this girl, Julia Bone, who was their leader, and she said to me one day that I looked really geeky.

"D'you know that? You look like a total nerd. *Are* you a nerd?"

I suppose I probably am, cos instead of saying something back to her, such as, "You look like a horse" (which she does, with those huge great teeth of hers), I just went bright red and didn't say anything, so that everyone tittered and started calling me Nerd or Geek.

I *know* if I'd told her she looked like a horse they would've respected me a bit, and might even have let me into their gang, but I always think of these things too late. At the time my mind just goes blank.

It was way back at the start of Year 7 when Julia Bone told me I looked like a nerd. All that term they called me names. Another one was Boffin. The Geek. The Nerd. The Boffin. I'd hoped they'd forget about it during the holiday, but we'd just gone back after Christmas and they were still at it. Yesterday I'd made a big mistake, I'd arrived before the bell had gone, and practically the first thing I'd heard as I crept into the playground was, "Watch it, Geek! You looking for trouble?"

I never look for trouble. I know they say you should stand up to bullies, but how can you when there's loads of them and only one of you? I think it's best just to keep out of the way.

I reached Mum and Dad's bedroom safely, without spilling any of Dad's tea, and pushed the door open with my bottom. Dad was propped up against the pillows, all ready and waiting. He said, "Thanks, Ruthie. That's my girl! How's school?" He talks in little bursts, all puffy and wheezy. He has this thing where he's short of breath. "School OK?"

I said that it was, because Mum is always careful to remind us that Dad mustn't be upset; and in any case, what would be the point? Dad couldn't do anything. You had to go where you were sent, and I'd been sent to Parkfield High.

"Lessons OK?" said Dad.

I smiled, brightly, and nodded.

"Learning how to be a doctor?"

I nodded again and smiled even more brightly. It's a kind of joke with Mum and Dad, me wanting to become a doctor.

"That's the ticket," said Dad. "Keep at it!"

Back in the kitchen, Sammy had poured milk all over himself and Kez was making a fuss because she said her toast was "burnded". She'll only eat it if it's, like, *blond*. Lisa was snuffling and wiping her nose on her sleeve. She's always snuffling – she can't help it. She has what Nan calls "a weak chest". But she doesn't have to wipe the snot off on her sleeve – that's disgusting! At the *breakfast* table.

"Where's your hanky?" I said.

"Haven't got one."

"Well, get one!"

"Don't know where they are."

"What d'you mean, you don't know where they are? They're where they always are! Th—"

"Oh, Ruth, just go and get her one!" said Mum. "And scrape Kez's toast for her while you're at it."

16

I'm frequently surprised that my legs aren't worn to stumps. I know Mum can't do everything, but I do occasionally wish that I could have been Child Number Two instead of Child Number One. I don't think that being Child Number One has very much going for it.

In spite of fetching hankies and scraping toast and collecting Dad's breakfast tray and getting the tiresome trio into their shoes and coats while Mum saw to Dad, I still managed to reach school before the bell. My stomach did this clenching thing as I turned into Parkfield Road and saw it there, waiting for me, like a great grey prison.

There's this wire mesh stuff over the windows, to stop them from being broken, and the walls are always covered in graffiti. Every term the graffiti's removed and every term it comes back again. I think some graffiti's quite pretty and I don't know why people object to it. But the stuff on our school walls is mostly just ugly, same as on our block of flats. If Mum'd seen them she would've known why I hated school so much, but Mum had enough to cope with, what with Dad, and work, and the tiresome trio, so she hardly ever went to parents' evenings. Actually, I don't think many other parents did, either. They would've found it too depressing, not to mention a total waste of time. You know those tables that they print, saying which schools have done best and which have done worst? Well, my school was one of the ones that did worst. It always did worst. It was the *pits*.

I was about to go slinking off down a side street and give the playground time to clear when someone called out, "Hi, Ruth! Wait for me!" and Karina Koh came huffing up the road. I obediently stopped and waited, cos it would've been rude not to, and also I wouldn't have wanted her to feel hurt, but I can't say that my heart exactly leapt for joy. Out of the whole year, Karina was the only one who called me Ruth (rather than Geek or Nerd) and the only one that ever wanted to hang out with me, so you might have thought I'd be a little bit grateful to her; maybe just at the beginning I was, when she first, like, came up to me in the playground and sat next to me in class. It's horrid being on your own and I did think that Karina would be better than no one. I even hoped we might become proper friends, but the truth is, I didn't really terribly like her. She'd been thrown out of Julia Bone's gang, which was why she'd latched on to me. She said we could be a gang all by ourselves. "Just the two of us! OK? And we'll take no notice of the others cos they're just garbage. They're all garbage, and we hate them! Don't we?"

She was always wanting me to hate people. Usually I agreed that I did, just to keep her happy, but it was a lie, cos I didn't. Not really. I hated *school*. I think perhaps I hated school so much that I didn't have any hate left over for actual people. Not even Julia Bone, who Karina hated more than anyone. She told me all sorts of things about Julia Bone.

"She *smells*. Have you noticed? I always hold my breath when I have to go near her. I don't think she ever has a bath. I don't think she even knows what a bath is for. She doesn't ever wash her hands when she's been to the toilet. I've seen her! She's *rancid*. She lives in a bed and breakfast. Did you know that? She has to live there cos her dad ran off. Her mum's, like, on drugs? She's a real junkie! And her sister's a retard. The whole family's just garbage."

Karina knew everything about everybody. But only *bad* things; that was all she ever told me. Like that morning, on the way in to school, when she told me that "Jenice Berry's mum's gone into the nut house." Jenice Berry was best friends with Julia Bone, so naturally Karina hated her almost as much as she hated Julia.

"They took her off last night. Came to collect her. She was raving! I know this cos we live in the same block."

She sounded really pleased about it. I said that it must be frightening, having your mum taken away, but Karina said that Jenice deserved it.

"They're all mad, anyway. The whole family."

Sometimes I thought that Karina wasn't really a very nice person. Then I'd get scared and think that maybe I wasn't a very nice person, either, and that was why nobody wanted me in any of their gangs, which would mean that I was even *less* of a nice person than Karina, since she'd at least started off in a gang. I hadn't even done that.

Other times I thought maybe Karina had only become not very nice because of everyone rejecting her, in which case I ought to be more understanding and sympathetic. So I tried; I really tried. I *wanted* us to be friends and she kept saying that we were, but every time I felt a bit of sympathy she went and ruined it. Like now when she said in these gloating tones that "People like Jenice Berry always get what's coming to them. Her and Julia Bone... they'll get theirs! It's only a question of time."

We walked through to the playground just as first

bell was going. Julia caught sight of us and yelled, "Watch it, Geek! We're out to get you! And you, Slugface!" I

won't say what Karina shouted back as it was a four-letter word, which I didn't actually blame her for as it's quite nasty to refer to a person as a slugface, even if they're not that pretty (which

21

Karina is not!). And I wasn't really shocked, which I would've been once. Everybody used four-letter words at Parkfield. All the same, I did wish Karina wouldn't answer back; it only made matters worse. Although maybe that's just me being a wimp. I suppose it was quite brave of her, really.

As we set off across the playground I caught sight of Millie, who used to be my best friend. I waved at her and she twitched her lips in a sort of smile but she didn't say hallo or anything. Her gang was one of the toughest. They weren't as mean as Julia's lot, but only because they would've thought it beneath them. They were, like, really superior. Like anyone that wasn't black wasn't worth wasting your breath on. It was hard to remember that this time last year me and Millie had been sharing secrets and going for sleepovers with each other. She wouldn't even give me the time of day, now. Nor would

Mariam, though I think Mariam would've liked to, if it hadn't been against the rules.

All the gangs had rules. The main one was that you didn't go round with anyone who didn't belong, which was why nobody went round with me – except Karina. Even the people that just hung out in little groups kept away from us; I dunno why. Karina said it was because I was a boffin. But I didn't mean to be!

The bell rang again. By now, the playground was almost empty.

"I s'ppose we'd better go in," I said. I didn't want to, but when it came to it I wasn't actually brave enough to do what some of the kids did and bunk off school. I think I still believed that school was a place where you might be able to learn something.

We trailed together across the playground and up the steps, keeping as far away from the rest of our year as we could.

The main corridor was full of bodies, all bumping and banging, and everybody shouting at the top of their voice. One of the teachers appeared at a classroom door and bawled, "Stop that confounded racket!" but nobody took any notice. A couple of boys barged into us from behind and a big yob called Brett Thomas caught my glasses with his elbow as he belted past. I went, "*Ow!*" I felt the tears spring into my eyes. It's really painful when someone smashes your glasses into your face. "That hurt!" I said. But I didn't say it loud enough for Brett to hear.

Karina said, "They're *animals*." But she didn't say it loud enough for Brett to hear, either. Not even Karina was brave enough to say anything to Brett Thomas. He'd told Mr Kirk, our class teacher, only yesterday, "No one messes with me, man!" and even Mr Kirk had backed down. Brett Thomas did pretty well whatever he wanted.

"He's on drugs," said Karina. "And his mother's a—" She put her mouth close to my ear. "*She goes with men.*"

I felt like yelling, "SHUT UP!" I didn't want to hear these things – not even about Brett Thomas. I didn't even know whether they were true. According to Karina, practically the whole of Year 7 was either on drugs or had mothers who were loopy or locked up or going with men, or fathers who had run away or drank too much or beat them. Some of them (according to

Karina) had fathers that were in prison. I wasn't sure that I always believed her. On the other hand…

Well, on the other hand, maybe she really did know these things. Maybe they were true and the whole of Year 7 was mad and dysfunctional, and that was why they behaved the way they did. It was a truly glum and gloomy thought and it filled me with despair. Sometimes I just couldn't see how I was ever going to survive another five years of Parkfield High.

But that was before Shay came into my life.

two

It was that same morning, when Julia yelled "Slugface!" at Karina, and Brett Thomas mashed my glasses into my face, that Shay arrived at Parkfield High.

Mr Kirk was at his desk, bellowing out names and trying to mark the register, which wasn't easy with all the hubbub going on. Brett Thomas and another boy were bashing each other in the back row, and some of the girls were shrieking encouragement. Mr Kirk would bawl, "*Alan Ashworth?*" at the top of his voice and someone thinking they were being funny would yell, "Gone to China!" or "Been nicked!" and everyone would start screeching and hammering on their desk lids.

Karina had told me last term that sometimes the teachers at Parkfield High went mad and had to be taken away in straitjackets, and for once I believed her. Well, almost. I didn't think, probably, that they went actually *mad*, but you could definitely see them getting all nervous and twitchy. Some of them got twitchy cos they were scared, like Mrs Saeed who taught us maths. She was so tiny and pretty looking, and Brett Thomas was like this huge great ugly hulk looming over her. I used to feel really sorry for Mrs Saeed.

But Mr Kirk, he twitched cos he was frustrated. What he'd really have liked, I reckon, was to hurl things. Books and chairs and lumps of chalk. Only he knew that he couldn't – he could only hurl his voice, and nobody took any notice of voices, least of all Brett Thomas. Karina said that Mr Kirk went home and beat his wife instead, but I think she may just have been making that up.

Anyway. The door opened and Mrs Millchip from Reception came in. She had this girl with her and everyone suddenly broke off yelling and hammering and turned to look. Even Brett Thomas stopped bashing, just for a moment. Mrs Millchip walked over to Mr Kirk, but the girl stayed where she was, leaning inside the door, with her hands behind her back, and this kind of, like, *bored* expression on her face.

If she hadn't looked so bored and so... supercilious, I think that's the word, meaning above all the rest of us, like we were rubbish and she was the Queen of England (except the Queen would be more gracious, having been properly brought up). Even as it was, with this scowly kind of sulk, you could tell she was totally drop dead gorgeous.

She looked the way I look in my daydreams. Tall. (I'm short.) Slim. (I'm weedy.) Heavenly black hair, very thick and glossy. (Mine is mouse-coloured and limp.) Creamy brown skin and a face that has cheekbones, like a model, and these huge dark eyes. (My skin is like skimmed milk, plus I wear braces, not to mention *glasses*.)

Mrs Millchip left the room, but the girl just went on leaning against the wall. Into the silence, Mr Kirk bellowed, "This is Shayanne Sugar, who's just joined us. I'd like you to make her feel welcome." Just for once there wasn't any need for him to bellow, but I expect by now he'd forgotten how to talk normally. I didn't really believe that he beat his wife when he got home, but he probably did bawl at her. She'd say, "You don't have to shout, dear, I'm not deaf," and Mr Kirk would bellow, "**I AM NOT SHOUTING!**" Well, that's what I like to imagine.

He told Shay to find herself a seat, while he went on with the register. Immediately everyone lost interest and went back to what they were doing, which was having private conversations and rooting about under their desk lids, eating things, or, in Brett Thomas's case, bashing. Shay stood there, letting her gaze move slowly about the classroom, like she was summing people up, deciding which would be the best person to sit next to.

There were several spare seats as it was the second week of term and the people who usually bunked off had already started. There was a spare seat next to me, but I knew she wouldn't choose that one. Why would a person who looked like a model want to sit next to an insignificant weed with braces on her teeth? *And* glasses.

"Talk about picky," muttered Karina. (She was sitting next to me on the other side.) "What's her game?"

"It's important," I said, "where you sit."

There was a seat next to Millie, and another next to Jenice Berry. I'd choose Millie any day, but that's because she used to be my best friend. The new girl might look at her and think she was just someone who was a bit plump and podgy and go for Jenice, instead. She wouldn't know that Millie was clever and funny, and that Jenice (in spite of looking like an angel) was as mean as could be.

Karina was still buzzing in my ear. "Why's she started so late, anyway? Why didn't she come at the beginning of term?"

I never really found out why Shay started so late. There were lots of things about Shay I never found out. Of course, she *might* go and sit next to one of the boys, if she wanted to be different. I wouldn't! But then I spend my life trying not to be different. Unfortunately it seems that I just am. I hate it! All I want is to blend in and be the same as everyone else. I don't know why I can't be, but it's always like there are people going, "Oh, *her*," or, "Well, of course, *Ruth Spicer*." Like, *she would, wouldn't she*? You have to be bold to enjoy being different. Like Shay. Shay was the boldest person I've ever known.

Just for a second, her eyes met mine and my heart went bomp! inside my ribcage. I really thought she was going to come over and sit by me. But she didn't. Instead, she stalked off to the back row and settled herself in solitary splendour, not next to anybody. The nearest person was Brett Thomas, right at the far end. The rest of the row was empty, as Mr Kirk had made  everyone move further down to the front. (Everyone except Brett Thomas. Nobody moved him anywhere.)

I waited for Mr Kirk to tell Shay to come closer, but he was still busy bawling his way through the register and didn't seem to notice. Karina sniffed and went, "Huh! Who's she think she is?" I didn't bother answering. I was thinking to myself that once Shay got put in the register we *would* be next to each other... Ruth Spicer, Shayanne Sugar. I wondered if Shay would notice this and think it was neat. Sugar, Spicer: Sugar and Spice! It made us sound like a TV programme!

Our first class that day was English, with Mr Kirk. After he'd banged on his desk with a book and got a bit of peace and quiet, he started handing back last week's homework, which was an essay on "The Night Sky". As usual, most people hadn't actually done it. When Mr Kirk demanded to know why, one of the boys said he couldn't be bothered, another said it was a waste of time, and Arlon Phillips, the boy who'd been fighting with Brett Thomas, said what was the point? Brett agreed with him. He said that it was a girl's subject, anyway.

"What's to write about? *The night sky is black. Wiv stars. And sometimes the moon, when it ain't cloudy.* That's about all there is to say."

"So why didn't you say it?" said Mr Kirk.

"Just have," said Brett.

"Would it have been too much trouble to write it down?"

Brett said yeah, it would. "I don't do homework, man."

"Well, I'm happy to tell you," said Mr Kirk, "that some people do. And that some people have found rather more to say on the subject than you have. For instance, how about this from Ruth Spicer—"

Oh, horrors! He was going to read it out! This is

what I mean about being different. I don't *ask* for my essays to be read out. I don't want them read out! Already I could hear the sounds of groaning. *That Ruth Spicer! There she goes again.* I knew if I turned round I'd see hostile eyes boring into me.

"Ruth has very creditably managed to write two whole pages," said Mr Kirk.

Oh, no! *Please.* I felt myself cringing, doing my best to burrow down into the depths of my prickly school sweater.

"I'll give you just two examples of imaginative imagery... *the clouds drifted past, like flocks of fluffy sheep.*"

Behind me, Julia made a vomiting sound. *Pleeurgh!* Jenice Berry immediately did the same thing. I could feel my cheeks burning up, bright red and hot as fire. Please let him stop! Why did he have to do this to me?

"The other example," shouted Mr Kirk, above the rising din of sniggers and vomits, "**ARE YOU LISTENING?** *The moon hung in the sky, like a big banana.*"

It sounded completely stupid, even to me. I'd been so proud of it when I wrote it! I'd thought it was really poetic. Now I just wanted to curl up and die.

"Moon's not a *banana*," yelled Julia.

"Can be."

Heads all over the room turned, in outrage. Who would ever dare contradict the great Julia Bone?

"Crescent moon," said Shay. "That's a banana."

Julia glared and muttered. Mr Kirk said, "Precisely! Very nice piece of writing, Ruth." (Cringe, cringe.) "As for the moron who wrote this—" He held out a sheet of paper with just the one line on it. *"The night sky is too dark to see."* He scrunched the paper into a ball. "I have only one thing to say to you, and that is, *grow up!*" And then he handed me back my essay and said, "Excellent!"

When I was at juniors I would've prinked and preened all day if Mrs Henson had said excellent. But at Parkfield High it wasn't clever to be clever. It was just *stupid*. Now they would call me names even worse then before. I could already hear the two Js, sitting behind me, making bleating sounds under their breath.

"Ba-a-aa, ba-a-aa!"

I did my best to ignore them, but I'm not very good at blotting things out, I always let them get to me, and then I want to run away and cry. Fortunately I do have a little bit of pride. Not very much; just enough to pretend that I don't care, or haven't noticed. I'd be too ashamed to let my true feelings show in front of people.

At the end of the lesson Mr Kirk set us some more homework. The subject was: My Family. He said he wanted it in by the day after tomorrow.

"Thursday. OK? I will accept no excuses! Anyone says they forgot and I shall send them for a brain scan. You have been warned!"

I muttered, "Send some people for a brain scan and you wouldn't find any brain."

I know it wasn't very nice of me, since people can't help not having any brain, any more than I can help having to wear glasses, but I don't think it's very nice to make fun of someone who's just trying to fit in and be ordinary. I didn't *ask* Mr Kirk to read out my essay. Unfortunately, Karina caught what I'd muttered. She gave this huge shriek and swung round in her desk.

"D'you hear what she said? *Send some people for a brain scan and you wouldn't find any brain!*"

If looks could have killed... well, I'd be dead, and that's all there is to it.

"Big banana moon!" said Julia.

"Ba-a-aa," went Jenice.

They carried on all through break.

"Why d'you have to go and tell them?" I said.

Karina tossed her head. She hates anything that she thinks is criticism.

"Not much point saying things if you don't say them to their faces!"

I expect she was probably right; I just wasn't brave enough.

"Look," said Karina, "there's the new girl."

Shay was leaning against the wire mesh that fenced us in. As well as wire mesh we had big gates with padlocks and brick walls with bits of broken glass on top. Most schools have security to keep people from getting in, but at Parkfield they had it to keep us from getting out. Well, that's my theory.

"Look at her! What's she doing?"

Shay was just watching. I saw her eyes slowly swivelling to and fro, same as they had in the classroom. She caught me looking at her and I very hastily turned the other way and began to study some interesting clouds that were drifting across the sky. They did look like sheep. *Flocks of fluffy sheep.* I felt my cheeks begin to burn all over again. If Mr Kirk was going to keep singling me out I'd just have to stop doing his stupid homework. Either that or do it so badly-on-purpose that he'd be rude about it and treat me the same as everyone else. One or the other. But I couldn't go on being humiliated!

The bell rang and we trundled back into school. First lesson after break was maths, which isn't one of my favourite subjects, though I do work quite hard at it, as far as you *can* work hard at Parkfield High. I used to think that I'd need it if I was going to be a doctor, cos of having to measure things out and knowing how much medicine to give people; but in fact, after one term at Parkfield I'd pretty well given up on the idea of being a doctor. I could understand a bit better why Mum and Dad had laughed when I'd first told them. Dad had said, "Well, and why not be a brain surgeon while you're about it?" Mum had said that I could always be a nurse. But I didn't want to be a nurse! I wanted to be a doctor. Well, I *had* wanted to be a doctor. Now it seemed more likely I'd end up in Tesco's, with Mum. But I still struggled and did my maths homework.

At least Mrs Saeed never embarrassed me by making comments in front of the class. Even when I'd once – wonder of wonders! – got an A-, she just quietly wrote "Good work!" at the bottom and left me to gloat over it in private.

Most people crammed as far back as possible for maths classes because Mrs Saeed was too nervous to make them move closer. Me and Karina were the only people in the front row. We didn't *have* to sit in the front row; there were empty desks in the row behind. But I liked Mrs Saeed and it seemed really rude if nobody wanted to sit near her. She might wonder why not and start to think that there was something wrong with her. It's what I would think, if it happened to me.

Shay didn't arrive until the last minute. This was probably because no one had bothered speaking to her, or told her where to go. *Including me.* I told myself that it was because she looked so superior and, like, forbidding, but really it was because it had never occurred to me. Even if it had, I still wouldn't have done it because I'd have thought to myself that I was too lowly and unimportant to go up and start talking.

"Here's Miss High and Mighty," hissed Karina. "D'you think she's looking for her throne?"

She was looking for somewhere to sit. Her eyes

flickered about the room, as they had before. And then, to my surprise and confusion, they came to rest on *me*. Next thing I know, she's plonking herself down at the desk next to mine. She said,

"Maths, yeah?"

I said, "Y-yeah."

"My favourite subject, I don't think!"

"Mine neither," I said.

"Well, there you go," said Shay. "That's one thing we got in common."

I was, like, really flattered when she said that. I couldn't have imagined having *anything* in common with someone as bright and bold as Shay.

After maths we had PE, in the gym. PE was one of those lessons that I absolutely dreaded, the reason being I'm just *so bad* at it. Karina was every bit as bad as I was, which meant we usually spent our time skulking in the corner, trying not to be picked on, while people like the two Js barged madly about, swinging to and fro on the ends of ropes and hanging off the wall bars, shrieking. Today, Miss Southgate, our big beefy PE teacher, made us all jump over the horse thingy. Oh, I hate that! I really hate it!

I always end up bashing myself or going *flump* across the top and not being able to get over. And then everybody sniggers and Miss Southgate tells me to try again.

"And this time, take a real run at it!"

So I do, but it isn't any use cos I still can't get over. Most probably what I do is catch my foot in the edge of the coconut matting and go sprawling on my face.

And then my glasses fall off and I hear them go *scrunch* underneath me, and Miss Southgate sighs and says, "All right! Next person." If the next person is Karina, she'll go flump just like I did. But if it's the two Js, they'll go hurtling over with about ten metres to spare *and* land on their feet the other side.

Until now they'd always been the star performers when it came to PE; them and a girl called Carlie who was in Millie's gang. They all belonged to the junior gym team and could bend themselves double and walk on their hands and balance without any signs of wobble on the parallel bars. Karina, in her sniffy way, said who'd want to?

"It's just stupid! Just showing off."

I didn't say anything to Karina, cos she'd only have got the hump with me, but I'd have given anything to be able to show off. Sometimes I had these dreams of hanging at the top of a rope, right up near the ceiling, and everybody being madly impressed and going, "Look! Look at Ruth!" Unfortunately I'm scared of heights, so it wasn't really very likely to happen. All I could do was watch, in a kind of awe. I wouldn't have minded if I never got an A- again, if I could only have whizzed up a rope or done the splits, like Julia. Cos she was absolutely THE BEST, it has to be said.

Until now. I couldn't believe it when Shay started up. She'd been doing her leaning thing, against the wall bars, silently observing everyone. And then it was her turn to run at the horse and she just, kind of, loped up to it, sailed over like it wasn't even there, and did a somersault with a handspring on the other side to finish off.

Everyone gaped, including the two Js. Karina muttered, "Who's she think she's impressing?" but it wasn't like Shay had done it to impress; more like it was just something that came naturally to her. "This is the way you jump over a horse." I got the feeling she didn't care one way or the other what anyone thought of her. She was Shay, and that was how she was, and they could take it or leave it. Which is the way that I'd love to be!

Afterwards, as we were leaving the gym, I heard Miss Southgate talking to her.

"Well," she said, "it looks as if we have a new recruit for the gym team! How about it? Would you like to join us?"

To my utter astonishment, Shay shook her head and said no. I couldn't believe it! How could she say *no*, just like that? To a teacher! I could tell Miss Southgate wasn't pleased. She said, "Well! That sounded pretty definite," and her voice was all sharp and prickly. I thought Shay would apologise, but she didn't; she didn't say anything. I asked her later – I mean, like, weeks later – why she hadn't wanted to join, and she just said, "Not worth it." She was such a mystery!

That evening, after tea, I shut myself away in the
kitchen to do my homework. The kitchen was the only
place that was warm enough since the central heating
had been turned off. Mum said we couldn't afford to
heat the whole flat, so now we just had it on in the front
room, but I was allowed to have the oven on low in the
kitchen. It wasn't exactly quiet out there cos I could
hear the television blaring in the next room, and the
person in the flat that joined ours had music on, really
loud, but I didn't mind that so much as the way Sammy
and the girls kept crashing in and out.

"We're playing!" yelled Lisa.

When I complained to Mum she said that it was nice the girls played with their little brother, and then she sat herself down at the kitchen table to ring one of my nans on her mobile. They started to talk and I really couldn't concentrate cos of listening to what they were saying. After a bit Mum put her hand over the mouthpiece and whispered, "Get Sammy off to bed for me, will you? There's a good girl!"

Well. That was easier said than done. It wasn't a question of "just getting him off to bed". First you had to catch him. Then when you'd caught him you had to fight to get him out of his clothes and into his pyjamas, and then another fight to get him to clean his teeth, and another fight to actually persuade him into the bedroom. (Actually Mum and Dad's bedroom, as we only have the two.) I finally got back to the kitchen to find that Mum was now working her way through a mound of ironing.

"If you did that in the other room," I said, "you could watch television at the same time."

"Too much hassle," said Mum. "Go on, you can work, I won't interfere with you."

I took out a sheet of paper and wrote MY FAMILY in big letters across the top. What could I write about my family?

"Look at this!" Mum was holding up one of Lisa's school blouses. "What on earth does she get up to?"

I nibbled the top of my pen, searching for inspiration. (*Bang*, went Mum, with the iron.) Maybe I could just write one line, like the person that wrote about the night sky.

"*My family is so ordinary I cannot think of anything to say about them.*"

Then Mr Kirk (*bang, thud*) would read it out and tell me to grow up and everyone would laugh, only they wouldn't be laughing because I was a geek or a boffin, they would be laughing because I'd dared to be cheeky. They might even start to respect me a little.

What if I did the spelling all wrong, as well?

"*My famly is so ornry I cannot thing of anythink to say abowt them.*"

Yess!!!!

"Know what?" said Mum. "This iron's giving out."

"*They are jest to bawrin for wurds. Wurds canot discribe how bawrin they are.*"

I was really getting carried away, now.

"*My mum is bawrin my dad is bawrin my sistus is bawrin my b—*"

"Well, that's it," said Mum. "That's the iron gone."

"*—my bruthr is bawrin. This is an eggsample of the bawrin things that happen in my famly. My mum has*

jest sed to me that the ion has gon but she duz not say
were it have gon. Maybe it have gon to the Nawth Powl.
Maybe it have gon to Erslasker. I wil aks her. Were has
the ion gon, I wil say."

"What are you talking about?" said Mum.

"The iron," I said. "Where's it gone?"

"What d'you mean, where's it gone? It's broke! Why
don't you make us a cup of tea and bring it in the other
room? You've done enough scribbling for one night."

I made the tea, but I didn't go into the other room. I
stayed in the kitchen, writing my essay. I found that
once I'd got going, my pen seemed to carry on all by
itself and I just wrote and wrote, making up all these
funny spellings. *Tellervijun* and *sentrel heetin* and
emferseema, which is what my dad has got that makes
him run out of breath. (It's really spelt *emphysema*. I
learnt it, specially.) In the end, I wrote five whole pages!
Even longer than my essay about the sheep and the
bananas. I felt quite proud of it.

But then, guess what? I got cold feet! I woke up in
the middle of the night and I knew I couldn't really
hand in five pages of silly spelling. I just wasn't brave
enough. But it was too late to write anything else, and
even if it wasn't I couldn't bear the thought of Mr Kirk
singling me out again. Specially not if it was about my
family. I'd just die of shame! So I tore up my five pages,
even though I thought they were funny, and on the bus

next morning, on the way to school, I wrote down my original sentence: "My family is too ordinary for me to say anything about them."

I wondered, as I got off the bus, whether Shay would sit next to me again. I did hope she would! It had made me feel a bit special, when Shay sat next to me. But I really couldn't think of any reason why she'd want to.

The Secret Writings of Shayanne Sugar

They are <u>PRIVATE</u>

KEEP OUT

This means you!!!

This school is a DUMP. The kids are RUBBISH. The teachers are PATHETIC. It is all GARBAGE.

Well it's OK, I won't be there for long. Not if I can help it! They're all a load of drivellers. Some stupid woman wanted me to join the gym team. Purlease! I'm not joining any of their ridiculous little teams, I'm not joining anything at all, NO WAY, full stop, finish. THE END. Sooner I get moved on the better. And I will! They'll soon get sick of me. BUT NOT HALF AS SICK AS I ALREADY AM OF THEM.

There's only one girl out of the whole stupid lot that's not a total thicko. Her name's Ruth and she looks like she's made of matchsticks.

Anything but a thicko! Ha ha. All the dorks and drivellers gang up against her, so I might kind of cultivate her and see what happens. Just out of interest. I certainly don't want her as a friend! Don't want ANYONE as a friend. I can manage on my own, I can! I don't need anyone. So I might not bother. I'll think about it.

Thinks...

I s'ppose it might give me something to do. Take away some of the boredom. WHILE I'M THERE. She hangs out with this girl that's a real slimeball. A right maggot mouth. But that's no problem! I can deal with her. She's just scum, like all the rest of them. Old Matchsticks has at least got a brain; sort of person

I could do something with. P'raps I'll give it a go. See what happens. If she's not interesting, I can always drop her.

The creep that takes English said to write an essay on My Family. What a stupid subject! My mum's a vampire. She sucks blood... yeah, and my dad's the invisible man!

One term. That's all I give it. After that – who knows? Maybe they'll just give up on me. Save us all a lot of grief.

Gonna write my essay now, about the vampire. Har har!

three

On my way into school next morning, I was ambushed by Brett Thomas. He must have seen me coming and laid in wait, cos he sprang out from behind a tree as I walked into the playground. It was quite scary. I jumped and gave this little pathetic bleat. Brett said, "Where ya goin', Goofball?"

I said, "Going into s-school."

I mean, where else would I be going?

"Wotcha got in yer bag?"

"N-nothing!" I clutched my bag very tightly with

both hands. "I haven't got anything in it!"

"Wotcha mean, you ain't got anyfink in it? Wotcha carryin' it for?"

"It's just *s-school* stuff." I cast round, desperately, but the playground was empty. I'd done my usual trick of arriving late, after the bell. It was just me and Brett Thomas!

"Give it us." He reached out and grabbed the bag from me. There wasn't anything I could do; I had to let him have it. Brett Thomas was a real hard nut, he'd bash your head in soon as look at you. Even Karina, who didn't mind giving a load of bad mouth to Julia Bone, wasn't bold enough to stand up to Brett Thomas. Nor was Julia, come to that. Nobody was.

"Wossis?" He'd pulled out my lunch-box and flipped off the lid. I watched as he prised up a corner of one of my sandwiches and sniffed at it. "Peanut butter? Man, that's some repulsive crap!"

All the food that Mum had put in my lunch-box went hurtling across the playground.

"What else yer got?"

"Nothing," I said. "It's just homework."

"*Homework?*" He upended the bag and shook out the contents. "Only nerds do homework!"

He was about to mash all my books and papers into the ground when a voice yelled, "You do that and I'll beat you to a pulp!"

It was Shay. I couldn't believe it! Shay, daring to threaten Brett Thomas... I felt like snatching up my stuff and making a run for it, but I knew I couldn't leave her there. She didn't know what Brett Thomas was like; she didn't know what she was letting herself in for.

"Honestly, it's all right," I said, "it doesn't matter, it's not important, it—"

"Course it's important!" She turned on me, fiercely. "Can't let people get away with this sort of thing!"

"So who's gonna stop us?" Brett brought his foot down on top of my maths book and began grinding it into the mud.

"I am," said Shay.

"Oh, yeah? You an' whose army?"

"Don't need any army!"

Shay launched herself at him.
He was bigger and
stronger than she
was, but she caught
him by surprise and
managed to throw
him off balance. I
hastily scooped up my
papers and rescued
my maths book.

"Come on," I said,
"let's go! Shay...
let's go!"

But she wouldn't. She stood there, glaring, hands on
hips.

"That is such *bad* behaviour," she said. "What are
you? Some kind of throwback?"

"*Please!*" I was hopping from foot to foot. There still
wasn't anyone else in the playground. "Leave him!"

"Next time," said Shay, "just pick on someone your
own size."

We turned, and walked off across the playground.
Brett came after us. He didn't actually do anything, just
fell in behind us, breathing over our shoulders and
uttering threats.

"I'll get you for this, bitch! You don't know who you're dealing with!"

Even now, Shay couldn't resist answering him back. "I know *what* I'm dealing with," she said. "Stone Age moron's what I'm dealing with!"

By the time we reached our classroom I had this great big tremble running through me, from top to bottom, making my whole body shake. I sank into my desk, next to Karina.

"You look really freaked out," said Karina. "Like you've been chased down the street by a horde of headless ghosts."

I told her it was worse than that. "Brett Thomas snatched my bag and Shay said she'd beat him to a pulp and he was a S-Stone Age moron!"

"What a total idiot." Karina craned her head to give Shay a contemptuous glare. (Shay had chosen to sit next to me, on the other side.) "Stupid thing to do!"

"Pardon me?" said Shay. She also craned her head. "You don't think it's right someone stands up to him?"

"Not unless they want to get themselves knifed," said Karina.

"He'd just better try it!" said Shay.

"You wait. You'll see! He'll get you."

"You shouldn't have done it," I said. "He's a horrible boy! He's been excluded once."

"Really?" said Shay, but she didn't sound too impressed.

"Yes, and then they went and let him back, and now he terrorises everyone."

Shay tossed her head. "Doesn't terrorise me!"

"But he's dangerous," I said. "He's really mean."

"So'm I," said Shay. "I'm meaner than a hyena! He's not gonna get me."

And he never did. I don't know what it was, whether he was scared of her, or whether he respected her, but after that he never came anywhere near her. He never came near me again, either, thanks to Shay. I don't know how it is that some people can stand up for themselves and beat the bullies and others can't. If I'd told Brett he was a Stone Age moron, I dread to think what he would have done. There was just something about Shay that warned people off.

When it came to lunchtime I didn't have anything to eat, on account of all my food being scattered over the

 playground. Karina, who also brought packed lunches, said that I could have half of one of her sandwiches, if I wanted, and a mouthful of yoghurt.

"But that's all, otherwise I'll get hungry, and if I get hungry I'll feel faint."

Shay then came over to sit with us, bringing a trayful of chips and curry, and a slice of cake.

"I tried to get two dinners but they wouldn't let me, but that's OK, we can share... look, I'll divide it up."

She actually drew a line with her knife down the middle of the plate and said that one half was for her, and the other half was for me. When I tried to thank her, she said I didn't have to do that.

"We're Sugar and Spice, right?"

She'd noticed! All by herself, without me telling her. Karina said, "What's that s'pposed to mean?"

"Means we share," said Shay.

"Why?" said Karina.

"Cos we do. Yeah?" Shay glanced at me for confirmation, and I beamed and nodded. I could see Karina was cross as hornets and didn't want Shay sitting with us, but it wasn't like her and me had sworn eternal friendship. We hadn't sworn any sort of friendship. We'd just drifted together out of convenience, cos being together had seemed better than being on our own. Maybe the three of us could form a gang. The Sugar and Spice gang!

It was a cosy idea, but I think I already knew that Shay wasn't a cosy sort of person.

We had two lots of homework that night: French and biology. I'm not terribly good at French, but I am good at biology! I love to find out about the body and the way it works, even though some of it is gruesome. The intestines, for example. All those metres of tubing, all pulsating away like crazy, gulping and squeeeeeeeeeezing, like a big sausage machine, as they move stuff along. It's really pretty disgusting if you stop and think about it. I mean, if all the time you're imagining to yourself what's going on inside you, all the gulping and the squeeeeeeeeeeezing and the sausage-making. After we'd learnt about it that morning I'd looked at Brett Thomas and wanted to giggle. The thought of Brett Thomas's innards! All churning about. Slurping and slopping and squirming like maggots. Ugh. Yuck. Totally gross!

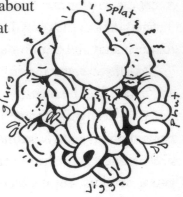

I said this to Karina and she squealed at me to shut up. She said if that was what went on inside us, she'd rather not know. But in its way it is actually quite fascinating, and especially if you're thinking that maybe one day you'll become a doctor.

Not that I was; not any more. People like me don't get to be doctors. Still, it didn't stop me being interested, and I'd been looking forward all afternoon to drawing my picture of the human digestive tract, which was what Mrs Winslow had set us. I sat down at the kitchen table with my felt-tip pens and began carefully to copy out the picture from the sheet she'd given us.

First there was the stomach, looking like a set of bagpipes. I did the stomach in yellow, cos I knew it was full of acid and yellow seemed like the right colour. Then a wiggly bit, which was the *duodenum*, which became the *jejunum*, which became the *ileum*, which all together made up the *small intestine*. I did those in green, as I thought that all the food that had been churned up by the acid might probably turn a bit greenish as it slurped on its way.

Next there came the *large intestine*, looping up one side and down the other, with a band across the middle. I made the large intestine big and bulgy, and I used a brown felt-tip pen for filling it in.

By now, my drawing was looking quite colourful; I just needed to say what everything was. I found a spider-tip pen and began to draw arrows and print duodenum and jejunum in tiny neat letters, being sure to check that I had the spelling right.

I'd just drawn an arrow pointing to the up bit of the large intestine and was about to write *ascending colon* when the kitchen door crashed open and Sammy burst through, shrieking, followed by Lisa and Kez. You'll never guess what! He went slamming straight into me, so that my pen scraped across the page, tearing up the

 paper and leaving a great furrow right through the middle of my beautiful drawing that I'd taken such care over. Oh, I was so angry! I bellowed at him.

"You stupid blithering idiot! Look what you've done!"

Sammy stopped and put his thumb in his mouth.

 "*Look!*" I snatched up the page and thrust it in his face. "See that? See what you've done? You've gone and ruined it! You stupid, thoughtless—"

"What's the matter?" said Mum, appearing at the door.

Sammy at once ran to her, sobbing. "What have you done to him?"

I said, "It's not what I've done, it's what he's done!"

"She yelled at him," said Lisa.

"Poor little mite! You've scared the life out of him."

"But he's ruined it! He's ruined my homework!" I was almost sobbing myself. My lovely intestines! I'd worked so hard at them. "It's taken me ages!"

"I'm sure he didn't do it on purpose," said Mum.

"They shouldn't be allowed out here when I'm doing my homework! Why can't they stay in the other room and watch television?"

"Don't want to watch television!" screeched Lisa.

"We've already watched it," said Kez.

Mum was peering over my shoulder at my poor mangled drawing. "Oh, dear! What a shame. Can't you do it again?"

"No! I haven't got time, I've still got my French to do."

"Why not use that one?" Mum nodded at the sheet Mrs Winslow had given us. "Why not just cut it out and stick in on the page, and then colour it?"

"Cos we're supposed to *copy* it!"

"That's a bit daft," said Mum. "That's a proper drawing, that is. Better than anything you could do. What's the point wasting your time trying to copy it?"

I said, "Why ask me?" And I crumpled up my spoilt drawing and hurled it across the room. I knew that Mum

was right, the drawing on the printed sheet was oceans better than the one I'd done, even with all my lovely bright colours and my little arrows. How should I know why Mrs Winslow wanted us to copy it? All I knew was that I'd enjoyed doing it and I'd been really pleased with the result and secretly hoping that perhaps I might get an A, or even an A+, and now it was totally ruined and I just felt *sick*.

"I'll take him away," said Mum. "Come on, Sammy! You come with your mum. Leave Ruth to get on with her studies."

I said, "It doesn't matter now, I've given up. I'm not going to bother any more."

"Well, I must say," said Mum, "I've never really seen why they have to give you all this extra work. You're at school seven hours a day. Isn't that enough?"

Mum went off, taking Sammy and the Terrible Two with her. I pulled my French book out of my bag and looked at it and put it back again. I'd given up! I wasn't bothering any more. Other people didn't bother; why should I? Nobody ever got into trouble. Now and again the teachers would mutter about "staying after school", but nothing ever came of it. I thought probably they preferred it if they didn't have too much homework to mark. I wasn't ever going to bother with homework again! What was the point, if I was just going to end up in Tesco's? I bet they'd never asked Mum if she'd got any GCSEs, and *she* was allowed to work on the *checkout*. I could do that! No problem. In any case, as Brett Thomas had said, only geeks did homework. I was through with being a geek!

Next day I told Karina that I wasn't bothering with homework any more. Karina said that she was glad. She said it was a great relief.

"It's not good if you keep getting things read out and teachers saying all the time how you've written loads more than anyone else and how you're just so *brilliant* and *wonderful* and—"

"No one's ever said I'm brilliant and wonderful!"

"No, but they keep going on about you... listen to

what *Ruth's* written, look what *Ruth's* done. It's not good," said Karina. "It just puts everyone's back up."

"Well, look at this," I said, and I showed her what I'd written for Mr Kirk. Karina read it and giggled.

"Hey!" She turned and grabbed at someone. It was a girl called Dulcie Tucker who was in Millie's gang. "Listen to what Ruth's written for Mr Kirk... *My family is so boring that I can't think of anything to say about them!*"

"Yeah. Right on," said Dulcie, like she couldn't have cared less.

I snatched the page back from Karina. "You don't have to go telling everyone," I said.

"Why not? It's funny! I hope he reads it out."

"So anyway, what about you?" I said. "Are you still going to do homework?"

Karina pulled a face. "I've got to. My dad'd bash me if I didn't."

"How would he know?" The teachers never sent notes home, or asked to speak to your parents. Not that I'd ever heard.

"He checks on me," said Karina. "He says he pays all

these huge amounts of tax so that I can get an education and he's going to make sure that I get one."

"Some hope at this school," I muttered.

"Yeah, well, I don't want one anyhow," said Karina. "Soon as I can, I'm getting out."

I asked her what she was going to do, but she said she didn't know.

"Don't know, don't care. Just so long as I can leave this dump."

I wondered what I'd do if my dad were like Karina's. Well, or my mum, since my dad doesn't pay any tax. He's on disability allowance. Mum pays! She's always going on about it. "All this money they take off me." Didn't she realise it was for me to get an education?

"Besides," said Karina, "it doesn't matter about me, cos I don't get up people's noses like you do."

"I don't mean to," I said.

"I know you don't *mean* to, but that's how it comes across. Always getting things right and knowing all the answers and sticking your hand up and doing your homework and – just everything!"

Humbly, I said, "I'll try and stop."

"Well, it'd be good," said Karina. "Cos then people wouldn't hate you quite so much and we might be able to join Amie Phillips and her lot. I could probably join them right now, if I wanted, but I wouldn't do it without you. It'd be nicer if we were together, wouldn't it?"

I said that it would, but really and truly I wasn't sure that I wanted to join Amie Phillips' lot. They were all remnants: all the leftovers that no one else wanted.

I didn't want to be a remnant! At the beginning of term I might have been desperate enough, but now there was Shay, as well as Karina, and I didn't feel quite so alone. I wasn't sure whether I could actually call Shay my friend, but she always chose to sit next to me, and sometimes she hung out with us in the playground (much to Karina's disgust). I don't know if she was jealous, or what, but she really didn't like Shay.

She used to hiss at me, like an angry snake. "Look at her! She's coming over – she's going to tag on to us. Get rid of her! Tell her to go away, we don't want her!"

I might have said, "Tell her yourself," but I didn't, just in case she took me up on it. I didn't want Shay to go away, I liked having her around – it made me feel safe and protected. I knew that all the time Shay was there, nobody would pick on me. Maybe after a bit, if I stopped showing off and sticking my hand up and being too much of a smart mouth, school might almost become bearable. Well, that's what I liked to think.

That weekend I helped Mum round the flat and played with Sammy and watched some television and didn't do any homework at all. Mum never said anything, like, "Don't you have any homework to do?" She never asked me about school; she was too busy working and looking after Dad. Dad sometimes asked me. He'd say, "How's school, then?" but I don't think he really wanted me to tell him. I usually just said, "'s OK," and left it at that.

I never saw Karina out of school. I could have done, cos she didn't live all that far away, but we weren't real proper friends. Not like me and Millie had been, or me and Mariam. I bumped into Mariam that weekend, when I went up the corner shop to get Dad's paper. We almost never spoke at school, but if we met outside we'd stop and chat. Mariam told me that her mum and dad were sending her away to live with her auntie. I said, "Oh, that's awful! Why are they doing that?" I mean, I love my aunties, all three of them, but I couldn't bear not to be with my mum and dad. I'd even miss Sammy and the Terrible Two!

I was all ready to sympathise, when Mariam said she was glad she was going to live with her auntie because it meant she wouldn't have to go to Parkfield any more. She said she'd be going to a much nicer school where there weren't any gangs and she wouldn't be bullied. I hadn't realised that she'd been bullied. I told her about Brett Thomas chucking my lunch across the playground, and the two Js calling me names, and she said that she hadn't realised that, either.

"If we'd all stuck together," I said, "it would've been all right."

Mariam told me that she'd only joined a gang because they'd threatened her.

"They said if I didn't join them I'd be one of the enemy... they said bad things would happen to me."

She promised that she'd call round when she came home for the half-term break, and we wished each other good luck. I went on my way feeling really depressed, even though I was happy for Mariam that she was going to a nicer school. She was such a sweet, gentle person. Not like me, always muttering cross things and frightening my poor little  brother and yelling at my sisters. I'd never heard Mariam yell, and I really hated the thought of her being bullied all this time and me knowing nothing about it. I did envy her, though, getting away from Krapfilled High.

On Monday, we had some of our homework back from the week before. I don't think Mr Abrahams even noticed that I hadn't done my French, but Mrs Winslow seemed a bit upset about not having any biology from me. She said, "I'm surprised at you, Ruth! What happened?" I mumbled something about my brother going and ruining my picture of the intestines and she said that was a pity but she really would like me to try and do it.

"It seems such a shame when your work is so good!"

Karina jabbed me with her elbow and pulled down the corners of her mouth. She herself had stuck the printed drawing into her biology book, like Mum had suggested I should do. At the  bottom Mrs Winslow had written, "This is not what I asked for." But she didn't suggest that Karina should do it again.

Next day, Mr Kirk handed back our essays on "My Family". I waited with bated breath to hear whether he'd read out what I'd written. I *wanted* him to read it out, to show people that I wasn't being a goody-goody any more. But he didn't! He didn't even comment. Not out loud. He commented on all the other essays that people had written. (*Some* people. A few people. There were only about ten.)

"Karina, I do think it would be rather nice if you were to consult a dictionary occasionally. All this fancy spelling makes it rather difficult to interpret. Or were you attempting a foreign language?"

"English," said Karina. (She has *no* sense of humour.)

"Really? Well, you had me fooled!" said Mr Kirk. "Shayanne... Your mother is a vampire and your father is the Invisible Man. Yes! Well. What can one say?" He tossed a wodge of pages on to Shay's desk. I stared at them in amazement. Shay's writing was very big and black and angry-looking. It was so big she hardly got more than about six words on a page. "Next time, perhaps, you might try using up a few less trees."

Shay said, "It all comes from sustainable sources."

"That may be, but the school still has to pay for the paper, so just concentrate on being a bit more economical. *Ruth*." He held out my one page; I took it. "This is disappointing. Please don't do it again."

That was all he said. I felt my cheeks burn just as fiercely as they had last week when he'd read out about the moon being a banana and the flocks of sheep. I felt so ashamed! Karina instantly slewed round in her desk and hissed, "Did you see what she wrote? *My family is so boring I can't think of anything to write about them!*"

She didn't impress anyone; the two Js just stared, stonily. And Shay was frowning. She was looking really ferocious. What was she so angry about? Who was she so angry *with*? I thought at first it was with Mr Kirk, because of what he'd said about using up less trees, but Shay never cared a fig what anyone said, least of all teachers. It was me! I was the one she was angry with! She was glaring at me like daggers might suddenly come shooting out of her eyes and make straight for me. I said, "W-what's the matter?"

"You," said Shay. "You're what's the matter!"

I said, "W-why? What have I done?"

"You know what you've done!"

I said, "What, what?"

Shay said that we'd "talk later". She said, "You've gotta get a hold of yourself... you can't carry on like this."

I just hadn't the faintest idea what she was talking about.

four

As soon as we got into the playground at break, Shay grabbed hold of me.

"OK! Time to talk."

"Bout what?" said Karina.

"Nothing to do with you! This is between me an' Ruth."

Karina tossed her head. "So what are you waiting for? Talk!"

"Excuse me," said Shay, "it happens to be private."

"Why?" I could see that Karina was working herself

up into a fit of jealousy. I could
sort of understand it. Shay was
a bit... well! In your face, I
suppose. "What's private
about it?"

"None of your business,"
said Shay.

Karina stuck
out her lower lip. She could be
really stubborn! Also, she's
quite thick-skinned, like she
was obviously determined to
stay even though Shay had made
it as plain as could be that she
wasn't wanted. I'd rush off immediately
if I thought I wasn't wanted; I'd be too ashamed to hang
around. But Karina wouldn't budge for anyone.

"It's rude to have secrets," she said.

"Yeah? Well, it's rude to pry into other people's
business. Just go away!"

"Won't!"

"You'd better," said Shay.

Karina gave a little swagger. "Or what?"

"You'll regret it, is what!"

Karina said, "Huh!" but I could tell she was starting
to have second thoughts. "I could go and join Amie's
lot," she said, "if I wanted."

"So join!" snapped Shay.

"I will, if you're not careful." Karina looked at me as she said it. "Is that what you want? You want me to go and join Amie's lot?"

I was beginning to feel a bit desperate. I didn't know what all this was about! "I'm sure we won't be long," I said. "Will we?" I turned, hopefully, to Shay, who still had hold of me. "We won't be long?"

"Dunno," said Shay. "Depends." She glared at Karina. "If some people would just let us get on with it—"

"Oh, don't worry! I'm going," said Karina. "I wouldn't stay here if you went on your bended knees and begged me!" And she flounced off across the playground to where Amie Phillips and her cronies were standing in a little huddle.

I wondered whether I'd mind if Karina joined them. I couldn't decide. I was too busy worrying about Shay and what she wanted to talk to me about. Why was she being so fierce? And what was so private?

"Right!" She gave me a little push. "What was all that with your homework?"

Stupidly, I said, "W-what homework?"

"Yeah, well, this is it," said Shay. "*What* homework? You never did any, did you?"

"I d-did my English," I said.

"One line! Call that an essay?"

"I couldn't think what else to write!"

Shay snorted. "Expect me to believe that? After all that you wrote last week? Moon's a banana and all that stuff?"

I hung my head, ashamed. "That was just stupid."

"It wasn't stupid, you mongo! It was clever. That's why he read it out."

"But I don't want him to read things out!"

"Why not?"

I mumbled, "Cos it makes people hate me."

79

"What *people*?" Shay's voice was full of scorn. "These people?" She waved a contemptuous hand at all the various groups and huddles in the playground. "Call that lot *people*? They're just mindless blobs!"

They might have been just mindless blobs, but they still called me names and made fun of me. And what did it matter to Shay, anyhow? I hadn't noticed her being so brilliant, what with calling her mum a vampire and using up all that great wodge of paper with hardly anything written on it. She hadn't even bothered to do her French, or draw the intestines.

I said this to her and she snarled, "We're not talking about me, we're talking about you!"

"But what does it matter?" I cried. "Nobody cares! What's the point?"

"I'll *tell* you—" Shay stabbed a finger into my breast bone "—what the *point* is." Jab, stab. "The *point*—"

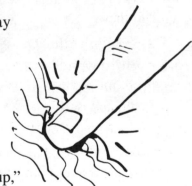

I went, "Ow! Stop it!" She was really hurting me.

"Well, then, just shut up," said Shay, "and listen!"

I said, "I'm listening."

"Right, then! You've got a brain. Yeah?"

I nodded, humbly. I knew I had a *bit* of brain, cos

Mrs Henson had told me so. Mrs Henson had said, if I worked hard enough I could pass exams, I could get to uni, I could be a doctor.

"So if you've got a brain, why not use it!" bellowed Shay.

I shrivelled. I did wish she wouldn't shout quite so loud.

"You want to end up like that lot?" Again, she waved a hand about the playground. "You wanna be pushed around for the rest of your life? Cos that's what'll happen. You let 'em get to you an' you'll be just another gawker like all the rest of 'em. Probably end up working in Tesco's."

I bristled at that. "What's wrong with working in Tesco's?" I wasn't going to tell her that my mum worked there.

"There isn't anything wrong with it," said Shay, "if that's what you wanna do."

"Well, maybe it is," I said.

"Yeah, and maybe it isn't," said Shay.

She had some nerve! "I don't see why you're going on at me," I muttered. "What about you?"

"Doesn't matter about me! I can look after myself. Don't see anyone pushing me around, do you?"

Humbly, I shook my head.

"So that's the difference between us. Yeah? It's why I can get away with it and you can't."

I thought, get away with what? But I sort of knew what she meant. Shay did her own thing, no matter what anyone said. When I tried doing my own thing, everyone jumped on me. What I couldn't work out was why it bothered her. Why should she care if I ended up in Tesco's? Why should I care, if it came to that? Mum was happy there. She had all her girlfriends, and they laughed and had fun. Of course it wasn't the same as being a doctor, but that was just a daydream.

"Oi!" Shay poked at me again with her finger. "You listening?"

I said, "Yes!"

"So you gonna do what I tell you?"

I sighed. "I s'ppose so."

"You better had!" said Shay.

I went back into class that day wondering how I felt about Shay bullying and bossing me. I decided that I didn't really mind. Which was strange, in a way, cos as a rule I get a bit stroppy if anyone tries telling me what to do, like with Millie and Mariam we never laid down rules or bossed one another. We got on really well! But with Shay it was like she'd set herself up as my own personal bodyguard. My minder! So long as I did what she told me, I'd be safe. I know it was a bit wimpish of me, but it did feel good to have someone on my side for once.

As soon as we were sitting at our desks, Karina turned to me and hissed, "What was all that about?"

I said, "Oh! Nothing, really. Just homework."

"What d'you mean, just homework?"

I smiled; a bit shamefaced. "Shay says I ought to do it."

"Why?" Karina's eyes narrowed to slits. "What's it got to do with her? I thought you were going to stop all the goody-goody boffin stuff?"

I said, "Y-yes. Well – maybe. I don't know!" I felt like a puppet, being jerked about in all different directions. "It's difficult," I said.

"You're just *weak*," said Karina. Fortunately everyone else was yelling at the top of their voice, so no one but me could hear her. "You just let her push you around! Don't blame *me* when everyone turns against you. I could join Amie's lot tomorrow, if I wanted. It's what I'll do," she said. "I will! I'll tell Amie we're not together any more."

We never had been together; not really. All the same, I hate upsetting people and I didn't want Karina to feel like I'd driven her away. I whispered, "I'll do my homework but I won't write stuff that's going to be read out."

"You'd just better *not*," said Karina.

"Well, I won't," I said. "Least, I'll try not to."

I added that bit to myself, very low, so Karina couldn't hear. I wasn't sure, if Mr Kirk set us an essay on something really interesting, that I'd be able to stop myself. Sometimes when I start writing I get, like, carried away, and that's when the flocks of sheep start appearing, and moons start turning into bananas.

There wasn't any problem with that night's homework cos all we'd had to do for Mr Kirk was read ten pages of *The Diary of Anne Frank*, and I'd already done that. I'd not only read ten pages, I'd read the whole book. I'd sat up in bed and finished it by torchlight, while the Terrible Two grunted and groaned and snuffled in their sleep. It was so funny in places, and so sad in others, that I couldn't tear myself away from it.

Even when I'd come to the end, I couldn't get to sleep for thinking about it. Imagining how it must have been, when the Nazis came. Imagining how it might have been, if they hadn't come. If Anne Frank had grown up and got married and had children of her own.

Karina said it was just utterly boring and she didn't know what people saw in it. According to Karina, if Anne Frank hadn't been discovered by the Nazis and sent to a concentration camp, no one would ever have bothered reading her stupid diary.

It was when Karina said things like that that I knew we couldn't ever be friends. I knew that if Mr Kirk had set us an essay on Anne Frank, I'd have dashed off ten pages of my own, just like that, and wouldn't have cared if Karina *had* gone off to join Amie Phillips. However, all we had for homework that night was maths. Oh, dear! I really have to concentrate *so* hard on maths. But I decided that I would. I'd make a determined effort, because dear Mrs Saeed never embarrassed me, or singled me out, even when I did get good marks. Also, of course, Shay would be pleased with me. I wanted Shay to be pleased. At any rate, I certainly didn't want her to be cross!

So after tea I cleared a space on the kitchen table and sat down with my maths book and started to concentrate. It was fractions, at which I'm quite hopeless. Especially *decimal* fractions. But I remembered Mrs Henson telling me: "You can do it, Ruth, if you just put your mind to it." That was fractions, too. I seem to have a big black hole in my brain when it comes to numbers. But I could do it!

I chewed the top of my pen. 0.35 + 0.712 + 0.9... I couldn't even use a calculator, cos my dear little brother had gone and ruined the only one we had. He'd dropped it in the  bath! Can you imagine? Mum said she'd see if there was another one on offer somewhere, like with a packet of crisps or something, but in the meantime I was having to work everything out *on paper*. In fact, that was what we were supposed to do anyway, but I bet nobody else did.

I'd just worked out the answer and was feeling rather pleased with myself, when Mum came bursting into the kitchen and cried, "Ruth, I've just remembered... it's Lisa's Home Bake day tomorrow and I promised her I'd make something for her to take in. I'd clean forgotten about it! Just pop down the corner shop, there's a good girl, and get me some pastry. I haven't got time to make any."

I hadn't got time to go down the corner shop. "I'm doing my homework!" I said.

"Oh, now, come on, it'll only take you five minutes!"

"So why can't Lisa go?" She was the one that wanted the stupid pie, not me.

"I'm not sending a nine year old out in the dark. Just get yourself down there and stop being so stroppy."

I went off, grumbling. How ridiculous, going to the corner shop for pastry when I had a mum who worked in Tesco's! Needless to say, there was a queue a mile long at the checkout. There would be, wouldn't there?

Everyone picking up fish fingers and TV dinners on their way home from work. Angrily I snatched a packet of pastry out of the freezer and stamped about at the back of the queue. Why did Mum do this to me? What about my education? I knew she had a lot to cope with, what with working all day and having to look after Dad, not to mention Sammy and the Terrible Two. But I was trying to do my maths homework!

Anyway, guess what? When I finally raced home with the pastry, it was THE WRONG SORT. She hadn't wanted *frozen* pastry.

"How can I roll it out if it's frozen?"

She sent me all the way back again. This time, for *chilled* pastry.

"Short crust, mind, not puff!"

So then I had a bit of an argument with the man at the checkout cos he said the frozen pastry wasn't properly frozen any more and he didn't want to take it back. But Mum hadn't given me any more money and I was practically in tears, cos I just couldn't stand the thought of going all the way home and all the way back for the second time, but in the end a nice lady standing behind me said it was all right, she'd take the frozen stuff, and I was just *so* grateful to her.

"That's better," said Mum, when I'd panted up six flights of stairs and back into the kitchen. (The reason I'd had to pant up the stairs was cos the lifts weren't working. *Again*.)

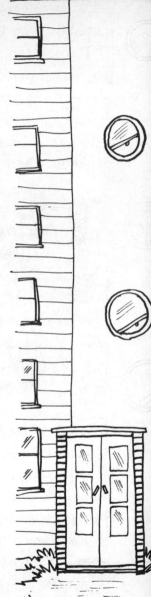

"Now, look, just pop across the hall and ask Mrs Kenny if she's got a tin of cherries I could have. Here! You can give her this in exchange." She tossed a tin of fruit salad at me. "Go on! I can't make a pie out of fruit salad."

I *hate* having to go and ask Mrs Kenny for things. Mum's always making me do it. I just find it so degrading! Anyway, Mrs Kenny didn't have a tin of cherries. I told her Mum wanted to make a pie for Lisa's Home Bake, so she gave me some sticks of rhubarb instead. I loathe rhubarb; so does Lisa. Tee hee! I should care. Mum did, though. She said, "What's this? Rhubarb? That's no good! I wanted cherries. You know Lisa won't eat rhubarb!"

"That's all she had," I said.

Mum made an impatient tutting sound, like it was my fault Mrs Kenny didn't have spare tins of cherries in her cupboard. Why didn't Mum, if it came to that? What's the point of working in Tesco's if you can't stock up with things?

"We'll have to cook it," said Mum. "Get me a saucepan. Well, go on! Don't just stand there. Do something!"

So before I know it, I'm over at the sink scrubbing rhubarb and chopping it into little pieces and pulling off the stringy bits, and dumping it in the pan and showering sugar over it.

"Not that much!" screamed Mum. "God in heaven, your dad won't have any left for his tea!"

I sometimes think that my mum is *seriously* disorganised. Me, myself, I like things to be orderly. I'm always tidying my desk and making out lists of Things to be Done. But it seems like I'm the only one in my family.

After I'd helped with the pie and done the washing up, including all the stuff left over from earlier, Mum said we might as well get the lunch-boxes ready for tomorrow.

"Save the rush in the morning."

I said, "*Mu-u-um*, I'm trying to do my homework!"

"Oh, very well," said Mum. "If you don't want to help. As if I don't have enough to do! I'd *hoped* to be able to put my feet up at some stage."

I looked at Mum and she did look frazzled. I know it wears her out, all the work she has to do. So we made up the lunch-boxes and I did some more washing up, and then, because poor Mum was obviously worn out, I told her to go and sit down and I'd make her a cup of tea; but when I took the tea into the other room I found her struggling with Dad's oxygen cylinder, trying to

drag it out from the bedroom. I ran straight over to help her. Dad's oxygen cylinder, which he has to use if his breathing gets extra bad, is really really heavy. Between us, we managed to lug it across the hall and into the lounge. We were both panting, though not as much as Dad. I suppose I ought to be used to it by now, but I'm always secretly terrified that maybe one day he just won't be able to breathe at all.

Naturally, with all the racket going on, Sammy woke up. He came pattering out in his pyjamas, wanting to know what was happening. Seconds later, the Terrible Two appeared. By the time I'd got them all back to bed, and Dad was breathing better with his oxygen mask, it was nearly ten o'clock and I was just feeling too tired to concentrate on fractions. The homework had to be handed in next morning. What was I going to tell Shay???

Secret Writings of Shayanne Sugar

Today I told that Karina girl where to get off. Some people just can't take a hint, I had to yell at her in the end. Then you should have seen her go! But really she must have a hide like an elephant. You tell a person to shove off, you can't make it much plainer.

SHOVE OFF YOU DORK YOU'RE NOT WANTED!

She's still hanging around, but I reckon she's starting to get the message. If she hasn't gone by the end of next week — well! She'll get what's coming to her.

Had a long talk with Spice. Told her to pull her finger out and stop trying to bring herself down to the same level as the rest of the morons. What's it matter if they call her names? Names can't hurt you. Anyway, they won't be calling her anything so long as I'm here. Anyone calls her names while I'm there, they'll get my fist in their gob. Yeah, and that includes Brett Thomas. What a gorilla! And that stupid

Joolyer and her sappy little friend. Prinking and prancing. I told Spice, they're just a load of dumbos. She's gotta get her act together! She said she would, but she's not gotta lotta bottle. God knows what'll happen when I'm not there. Still, that's her problem. She'll have to learn to fight her own battles – I can't be around all the time.

I dunno why I bother, really. What's it to me if she ends up like the rest of 'em? Be easier just to let her get on with it. She's nothing to me! This time next year I won't even remember who she was. But I just CAN'T STAND IT when a load of mindless blobs go round guzzling and slurping and GOBBLING UP anyone that's got a bit of brain. It DISGUSTS me, to tell the truth. That's why the Karina girl has gotta go. Not just cos she's in the way, though she is in the way (but not for long. I got her number!) but because

she's like a leech. Except instead of sucking blood, she sucks brain. I've watched her! She thinks it's really funny when Spice turns in one line of homework and calls it an essay. Yay! That's great! That's really amusing, that is. Another bit of brain down the toilet. If she had her way, she wouldn't stop till she'd sucked the lot out, and then there'd be one more mindless blob cluttering the place up and thinking it's clever to be stupid.

GOD THEY MAKE ME SICK.

The Vampire's gone off for three days on a training course. She says it's to do with cosmetics. Oh, yeah? More likely a course on How to Put your Fangs to Good Use, or How to Avoid Garlic. In other words, a vampire convention! That's what I reckon. There'll be all these other vampires there, all sharpening their fangs and thirsting for fresh glasses of blood. I asked her if she was taking her coffin with her and she said, "What on earth are you talking about?" She said I had a very morbid sense of humour. "If it is a sense of humour. Honestly, Shay! Do you have to be so ghoulish?"

Yup! I have to be. It's the only way I can get by.

The Vampire went off yesterday. She thinks the Invisible Man is then here keeping an eye on me, but if he is I can't see him.

"Hi, Dad! You there? Anyone at ho-o-o-o-me?"

No reply. I don't think he came back last night. At any rate, his bed wasn't slept in. I've checked the answerphone, but there's no messages. Nothing on the email. I've tried ringing his mobile, I've rung it several times, but it always seems to be switched off. Maybe he's gone on a training course, too. How would the Vampire know? They never talk.

I remember the first time they left me, I was scared. I stayed in my bedroom and cried. Boo hoo! So pathetic. Course, I was only nine years old. I couldn't give a toss now. What do I care?

It's odd he hasn't even left a message. I s'ppose he's all right. I s'ppose he hasn't had a car crash or anything. Nah! Course he hasn't. The police would have been round. It's what they do, they come and tell you. He probably thinks the Vampire's here. He thinks she's here, she thinks he's here.

GOD THEY'RE SO USELESS!

five

I desperately didn't want to wake up next morning. Mum had to come and bawl at me three times. *"Ruth, I'm not telling you again!* Get out of that bed! And get your sisters up. Do you want to be late for school?"

I didn't just want to be late. Being late wasn't enough. I didn't want to go *at all*. I was just so scared that Shay was going to be angry with me! It wasn't that I thought she'd bash me or anything. But she'd give me that *look*, like I was lower than an earthworm. Like she didn't know why she'd ever bothered.

"Just a mindless blob!"

Shay despised mindless blobs. I didn't want to be one of them. I didn't want her to despise me – I wanted to be someone worth bothering with!

I crept into class just as Mrs Saeed was collecting homework.

"Ruth," she said, "just in time!" And she smiled at me and held out her hand, with this really happy expression on her face. "Homework?"

I mumbled that I was sorry, but I hadn't done it. Poor Mrs Saeed! She looked so disappointed, like I'd really let her down. She said, "That's not like you, Ruth." I hung my head and didn't dare look at Shay. As I slipped into my seat, Karina nudged me, like she was gloating, and went, "Hah!"

It was like she thought she'd scored some kind of victory. I wanted to turn my back on her, but that meant I'd be facing Shay. I grabbed my rough book and shielding it with my hand, cos Karina was really nosy, she always wanted to be in on absolutely everything, I wrote, "I couldn't help it, I had to do things for my mum," and pushed it across to Shay. Would she write back to me???

She did! She wrote, "**WHAT THINGS?**"

I waited till Mrs Saeed was chalking stuff on the board, then whispered, "She made me go down the shops, *twice*, and then she made me go and borrow some rhubarb from Mrs Kenny, and then I had to help her make a pie, and then—"

Mrs Saeed turned round and I immediately stopped. I don't know why, since most everyone else was talking. People just talked all the time. If they weren't talking they were playing games or reading magazines. Brett Thomas was chucking things about the room, Dulcie Tucker was plaiting someone's hair, a girl called Livvy Briggs was painting her nails. But I guess I felt I'd already upset Mrs Saeed quite enough.

"Then what?" hissed Shay.

"Then... we had to get the lunch-boxes, and then I

did the washing up and made a cup of tea, and then Dad was taken bad and I had to help Mum with his oxygen, and then – then I had to see to the others, and – and by then it was time for bed!"

Shay went, "Hm!" She was looking at me, frowning, but not like I was an earthworm. More like I was... some kind of problem that had to be solved.

"Gotta get things sorted," she said.

At breaktime she told Karina to "Just go away and do something else. All right?" Karina turned an odd mottled colour, all red and blotchy, and shrieked, "Who d'you think you are, telling me what to do?"

Shay, in this really bored tone, said, "We've been through all this before."

"Yes, we have!" shrilled Karina.

"Well, then... just go away and leave us alone! This is between me and Spice."

I wanted to say that it didn't really matter if Karina stayed, but I knew that it did. It wasn't that we were having secrets, but it was definitely something private. Just between the two of us.

"You'll regret this!" Karina hurled it venomously over her shoulder as she stalked off. "You'll be sorry!"

It was me she was saying it to, not Shay. She knew Shay wouldn't care.

"Forget about her," said Shay. "She's rubbish! Tell me again why you couldn't do your homework."

I sighed. "Well, there was this Home Bake day at my sister's school—"

I went through it all, from the beginning. The pastry, the rhubarb, the pie, the lunch boxes, the tea, Dad's

oxygen. It all sounded completely mad! Well, it did to my ears. But Shay just listened, without saying a word.

"So then it was, like, ten o'clock," I said, "and I was just too tired!"

"Not surprised," said Shay. "Anyone'd be too tired."

I looked at her, gratefully. She wasn't mad at me!

"Does this sort of thing happen all the time?" she said.

I nodded. "Most of the time. See, my dad's got this thing where he can't breathe properly. Sometimes he has to have oxygen, and the oxygen cylinder's, like, really heavy? And Mum can't manage it on her own, so I have to help her, and then there's Sammy, he's my little brother, and Kez and Lisa, they're my sisters, and I have to help her with them cos she's got Dad to take care of, plus she goes out to work all day, so—"

"This is crazy!" cried Shay. "You ought to tell your mum that you've got homework to do."

"I have! But Mum doesn't believe in homework. She says we get too much of it. It's not her fault!" I was anxious that Shay shouldn't think badly of Mum. "It's just that she's so worn out, you know? She really needs me to help her."

"Yeah, but you really need to do your homework," said Shay. "Know what?"

I said, "What?"

"You oughta go to the library and do it."

I looked at her, doubtfully. Before Karina latched on to me I used to spend every lunch break in the library (except that it's actually called the Resource Centre and has more people using the computers than reading books) but no way did I want to stay on at school at the end of the day. I didn't want to stay on at school a minute longer than I had to! I said this to Shay and she said she wasn't talking about Krapfilled's library, she was talking about the *public* library.

Surprised, I said, "Do they let you?"

"Course they let you! What d'you think?"

I didn't know. I'd only ever been to the public library once, and that was at juniors, when Mrs Henson had taken us all on a class visit and had shown us how to borrow books. I'd asked Mum if I could have a ticket, but somehow we'd never got around to doing it.

"It's not right," said Shay, "not even having half an hour to do your homework. And look, just stop worrying about that stupid Karina." She'd obviously noticed my eyes straying across the playground, to where Karina was hovering on the outskirts of Amie Phillips and her gang. "She's not good for you – she'll just drag you down."

I said, "I know, but I wouldn't want her feelings to be hurt."

"You don't actually *like* her?" said Shay.

I wrestled with my conscience. I think it was my conscience. I felt that I ought to like Karina, seeing as we'd been sort of sticking together ever since half way through last term; but I kept remembering stuff she'd said, like for instance about Anne Frank, and I knew that I didn't really.

"You don't, do you?" said Shay. "You just put up with her. But she's a blob, same as the rest of 'em, and that's what you'll be if you don't junk her. You gotta think of yourself," urged Shay. "Won't get anywhere, otherwise."

I knew that Shay was right, though I still didn't want Karina's feelings to be hurt. She deliberately went to sit somewhere else for our first class after break and I must say it was a huge relief not to have her nudging and poking at me all the time, but she wasn't sitting anywhere near Amie, and that was a bit of a worry because what would she do if Amie wouldn't let her be part of her gang? She'd be on her own and then I'd feel dreadful.

I did my best to harden my heart, but it wasn't easy. Not even when I was leaving school that afternoon and Karina came up to me and hissed, "I hate you, Ruth Spicer! The only reason I ever hung out with you in the first place was cos I felt sorry for you, cos you're such a pathetic nerd!" I suppose I should have hated her back, but I knew what she was saying wasn't true. I don't mean about me being a nerd, but about that being the reason she'd hung out with me. She'd hung out with me because we were both on our own. Nobody wanted Karina any more than they wanted me. And now I had Shay and Karina didn't have anyone and I felt quite bad about it.

Next morning she still wasn't talking to me, and she didn't seem to be talking to anyone else, either. I did so wish Amie Phillips would let her join her lot! I didn't want to have her on my conscience.

I'd thought Shay might have forgotten her idea of me going to the library. I might have known she wouldn't. She said she'd been thinking about it and she'd decided I ought to go there straight away, after school, and get started.

"No time like the present," she said, in this bossy, grown-up way.

I told her, apologetically, that I couldn't do it that day cos my dad would be worried where I was. I always get home an hour before Mum and if I didn't arrive he'd think something had happened. Dad gets very wound up. I suppose it's because of not being well. Shay said, "Phone him!"

"I can't," I said. "I haven't got a phone!"

I'd once said this to Karina and she'd stared at me like I was something that had just crawled out of a pond. "You haven't got a *mobile*?"

I was so ashamed! I thought that Shay would stare at me as well, but she just shook her head, like "Stop making excuses!" and said, "Use mine. Here!" She thrust one at me. "Ring your dad and tell him."

"What, n-now?" I said.

"Why not?" said Shay.

I thought that Dad might be snoozing, or watching telly, but I wasn't brave enough to argue. Meekly I took the phone and dialled our number. Dad sounded puzzled when I said that I was going to the library to do my homework. He said,  "Why? What's in the library?" I explained that it was somewhere you could sit and work. Dad wanted to know what was wrong with sitting at home, so I mumbled something about the library being more peaceful, cos you weren't allowed to talk in there. That was what Shay had said.

"No one's allowed to talk, so you can just get on with things."

"Well, suit yourself," said Dad. "I don't know what your mum's going to say."

We had maths and French to do that night. I was quite nervous about going to the library. I kept asking Shay what you had to do. She said, "You don't have to do anything! Just go in and sit down."

She could obviously see that I was anxious, and maybe she thought that left to myself I mightn't ever get there, so in the end she said that she'd come with me.

"Just this one time."

I was humbly grateful as I knew that Shay lived way over the other side of town and it would take her for ever to get home.

"You'll be really late getting back," I said.

"So who cares?" said Shay.

"Well... your mum?" I said. "Won't your mum be worried?"

Shay tossed her head. "My mum never worries. She's not there, anyway."

"What, you mean... when you get back the flat is empty?"

"House. Yeah. 's empty."

I couldn't imagine getting back to an empty house. Well, I couldn't imagine getting back to a *house*, cos I've always lived in a flat. And there's always been someone there. When I was little it was Mum and now, of course, there's Dad. I asked Shay if she minded and she said no, why should she? She sounded a bit aggressive, like she thought I was being nosy, or criticising the way she lived, so after that I didn't say any more. I'd learnt that if Shay wanted me to know things, she'd tell me. If she didn't, there was no point in asking. She wasn't exactly secretive. Just, like, what she did was her business and no one else's, not even mine. She was looking out for me, but we still weren't proper friends. Not like I'd been with Millie and Mariam, when we'd all exchanged confidences and knew everything there was to know about each other.

Anyway, I was really glad that Shay had come with me as the library is this huge, important-looking building with great wide steps going up to it and a big green dome on top, so that if I'd been on my own I'd probably just have turned round and run away. But Shay marched in there as

bold as could be, with me creeping behind her, and
nobody stopped us or asked us what we thought we were
doing. Shay consulted a board which said *Ground Floor,
1ˢᵗ Floor, 2ⁿᵈ Floor*, etc.

"Children's," she said. "You don't want that!
It'll be full of kids. We'll go up to the Adults."

I wasn't sure that I wanted to go up
to the Adults, but she didn't give me
any choice, just dragged me on
to the escalator.

The first floor was full of tables and chairs, and racks of
magazines and newspapers. Grown-ups were sitting all
around, reading or writing and looking solemn.

"This'll do," said Shay. She very firmly led me over
to an empty table and sat me down. "There! Now you
can get on with things."

I squeaked, "You're not going?"

"Gotta get back," said Shay. "You'll be all right
here."

And she waltzed off to the escalator, leaving me on my own. It was a really bad moment. I was still expecting someone to come over and tell me that I wasn't allowed in the library all by myself, without a grown-up, and that I must go away *immediately*, but nobody did. Nobody took any notice of me at all. After a while I started to relax and concentrate on my homework, and oh, it was so lovely sitting there! I'd never been anywhere without noise or bustle. Without music or the telly, or Mum nagging at me to do things, or Sammy and the Terrible Two roaring in and out. I mean, just at first it was, like, a bit weird; I kept listening to the silence and wondering what was wrong, but once I'd got used to it I thought that this was how

I'd like to live. I'd have one room all of my own, with a table and chair and lots of bookshelves, where no one could come in without being invited, or at any rate asking permission. In other words, it would be totally, utterly and completely PRIVATE. And I'd get all my homework done with no trouble at all. Even maths. Even decimal fractions. Hooray!

Mum wasn't too pleased when I got home. She said, "Where have you been?"

I said, "In the library! I told Dad, I—"

"I know you've been *in the library*, but what for?"

"Doing my homework! It's quiet in there, I can get on with things."

Mum said, "I could've done with you getting on with a few things here!" She said how was Dad expected to cope, all by himself, when the Terrible Two got back and I wasn't there? "Seems to me your dad's health is more important than your homework! Who told you to go to the library, anyway?"

I said, "A girl at school."

"What girl?"

"New girl. Shay. She said the library was a good place to work in, and it is, cos I've done *all* my homework," I said, proudly, "and now I can help you!"

"Bit late for that," grumbled Mum, but she agreed that I could go to the library if I had to, so long as I was home by quarter to five. She still wasn't happy about it. She still didn't really see why I should want to go and shut myself away in "a stuffy old place like that" when I could be sitting here in the kitchen at home.

I said, "Mum, it's not stuffy! They've got computers and CDs and a coffee bar. And books, and newspapers, and—"

"Yeah, yeah," said Mum. "So who is this girl? *Shay?* What kind of a name is Shay?"

I said, "It's short for Shayanne."

"What, like she's a Red Indian or something?"

Shocked, I told Mum that people didn't refer to Red Indians any more. "They're Native Americans!" We'd learnt that in Juniors.

Mum said, "Whatever! Is that what she is?"

I said, "I don't think so."

"Well, whoever she is," said Mum, "she sounds like she's really pushing you around."

"I only do what I want to do," I said.

"Huh!" Mum obviously wasn't convinced. She said that Shay sounded like a bit of a bully. "Perhaps I'd better meet her. Why don't you ask her over?"

Me? Ask *Shay?*

"Well why not?" said Mum. "It's time I met some of your new friends."

"Yes, but—" Shay wasn't that sort of friend. "She lives in Westfield."

"So? If you're saying we're not grand enough for her—"

"It's not that!"

"She goes to the same school as you even if she does live in Westfield. What's she got to be snotty about?"

"She's not snotty," I said, but even as I said it, I thought to myself that I didn't actually know. I didn't actually *know* very much at all. But I did know that Westfield was posh, cos Mum always said it was. It was where Mum dreamt of moving to if ever she had a big win on the lottery. And if Westfield was posh, Ennis Road, where we lived, was the pits. How could I invite Shay to Ennis Road?

"It's been a long time since you had anyone over," said Mum.

Not since Juniors. But that had been different cos we all lived on the same estate. Millie lived in Archer Court, which was the big block of flats right opposite, and Mariam lived round the block, just five minutes away.

"Dunno how she'd get here," I said.

"Trust me," said Mum, "if they live in Westfield, they'll have a car. You ask her over for Saturday. I'll get something in for tea."

I really didn't think that Shay would want to come. I plucked up my courage and asked her in the playground at break next day. I said, "My mum said to invite you to tea, Saturday, but it's all right if you'd rather not." I knew she wouldn't just make an excuse, like anyone else would. She wouldn't pretend she was  going somewhere or had to see her nan or her auntie. She'd say, straight out, if she didn't want to come. I was just so surprised when she said yes!

"I'll get the Vampire to drop me off." She always called her mum the Vampire; I didn't like to ask why. "What time d'you want me there?"

That threw me into a fluster as I hadn't thought that far ahead. I said, "Um... 'bout two o'clock?"

And then immediately wished I'd made it later because what were we going to do from two o'clock until tea time? Shay wasn't the sort of person you could have cosy conversations with and I didn't fancy sitting down to watch TV. I hardly ever watch telly, as a matter of fact; only if there are hospital programmes. I like those! Unfortunately Dad says they "turn him up" so I can only watch if he's doing something else, which usually he isn't.

I told Mum I'd asked Shay for two o'clock and Mum said that was fine. "You can take the kids up the park."

"Mu-u-u-m!" I was horrified. I couldn't expect Shay to trail up the park with a bunch of snotty kids! But Shay totally astonished me, cos when she arrived and Mum said, "Well, now, how about you all getting out from under my feet for a bit?" she seemed to think it was quite a good idea.

And in fact it wasn't so bad as it at least gave us something to do. We went to the adventure playground and me and Shay sat on the swings while the others went on the kiddy slide and the roundabout and the dotty little climbing frame and kept out of our hair, except for Sammy falling over and hurting himself and bursting into loud bawling sobs, and then it was Shay who went over and picked him up and kissed him better.

"He's kind of cute," she said, as she came back.

"He's all right," I said. "But he's spoilt rotten cos he's the only boy. Are your mum and dad like that?"

"Like what?" said Shay.

"*Sexist.*"

Shay said, "Dunno. I expect so. Prob'ly. Most people are."

I don't quite know what we talked about as we sat on the swings. Shay didn't ask me any questions about myself and I didn't ask any about her, cos I had this feeling she mightn't like it, plus we weren't really what I'd call friends, at any rate not yet, though I hoped that we might be one day. We certainly weren't at the stage of swapping secrets or anything like that. Mostly at school I still hung out with Karina, except when Shay decided she wanted to talk to me, and then Karina would go off in a sulk. But you can't invite someone to tea and then spend the time in total silence, so I think most probably I just burbled. It's what I do when I get embarrassed. I open my mouth and words come streaming out, all hustling and jostling and banging and bumping, and I just don't seem to have any control over what I'm saying. I mean, I didn't particularly *want* Shay knowing all my great plans for being a doctor and how Mrs Henson had told me that I could do whatever I wanted if I put my mind to it. The idea of being a doctor now struck me as utterly pathetic, and telling her about Mrs Henson just seemed like boasting.

When we got home, tea was ready. Mum had made this huge effort and bought cakes and buns and biscuits, and sausage rolls and crisps and toffee pudding. Almost like a birthday party! She'd never laid on such a spread for Millie and Mariam. We all sat round the kitchen table, including Dad, and Sammy behaved really badly, snatching at food and upsetting his drink, and nobody doing anything to stop him, so that I felt really angry.

It wasn't fair! Just because he was a boy. At one point he picked up a sausage roll and chucked it at Shay, across the table. Even Mum thought that was going a bit too far. She said, "Sammy! Stop it!" but Shay just caught the sausage roll and chucked it straight back at him.

"Well!" said Mum, beaming. "You've obviously got a brother of your own!"

"*Have* you?" I said.

Shay shook her head. "Nope!"

"Sisters?" said Mum.

"Nope."

"Only child? Oh, dear! This lot must seem like a right handful."

Mum wasn't in the least bit shy of asking questions. Not even if Shay did live in Westfield. She even asked her what her mum and dad did. Shay said that her mum was a beauty consultant and her dad ran his own company.

"Ooh! That sounds important," said Mum.

"He sells *plastic boxes*," said Shay. She said it like he was selling maggots, or drain covers.

"But his own company!" Mum was impressed, I could tell. Dad asked how many people Shay's dad employed. Shay said, "Two."

"Well – still. He's his own boss," said Dad. "No one to tell him what to do."

Before he got his emphysema, Dad used to work on the buses. He was always complaining of people telling him what to do.

After we'd finished tea, Shay thanked Mum for inviting her and said that she'd be going now. I was relieved, in a way, cos although I'd quite enjoyed her being there I couldn't think what we'd have done next. I really didn't want to take her into my bedroom. It was just such a mess, what with Kez and Lisa's stuff all over the place. I would've been too ashamed. I try very hard to keep my bit clean and tidy, but it's quite disheartening. Sometimes I'm tempted to just give up. But if we didn't go into the bedroom we'd either have to sit in the kitchen, which would be boring, or sit in the other room and watch television, which would probably also be boring. I just *so* didn't want Shay to be bored!

Mum asked her how she was getting home. "Do you want to ring your parents and tell them to come and fetch you?" Shay said no, that was OK, she could find her own way.

"But it's going to be dark any minute," said Mum. "I really think you should ring."

But Shay wouldn't. I went down to see her off, and I thought that I'd be a bit scared going back across town in the dark.

"I do it all the time," said Shay.

I was about to ask her if her mum didn't worry, when

I remembered what she'd said, that her mum never worried. I said this to Mum when I went back upstairs.

"She's very independent," I said.

"Very self-possessed," said Mum, like being self-possessed wasn't a good thing. "I just hope she wasn't angling for us to take her home."

"She wasn't," I said.

"Well, too bad if she was. It's time she learnt that we can't all afford to run cars. I'm just surprised her parents are so irresponsible. Letting a girl of that age roam about by herself! And you needn't think you're going to start doing it."

"Mum, didn't you like her?"

"Not my cup of tea. Too sure of herself by half."

"She was nice to Sammy," I said.

Grudgingly, Mum agreed that she was.

"And she thanked you for inviting her!"

"Oh, yes, she remembered her manners," said Mum. "But there's just something about her... what happened to Millie? Why aren't you seeing her any more?"

"She's got other friends," I said.

"Well." Mum sighed. "Just don't let that Shay push you around, all right? Be careful! I'm not at all sure she's a good influence."

When I'm a mum, I'll *never* say that about my children's friends.

Secret Writings of Shayanne Sugar

The Vampire's back. So's the Invisible Man. They had a right slanging match when they discovered they'd both been away at the same time. It was like, "What is the MATTER with you? Why can't you ever comMUNICATE?"

"ME communicate? What about YOU?"

"I'd had that conference arranged for MONTHS!"

"So why the [swear words, swear words] didn't you [swear words] TELL me?"

"I did [swear words] tell you! You just never [swear words] LISTEN!"

After which we had a whole string of swear words. If I was putting little stars instead of actual words, the conversation would look like this:

**************** ******* **********!

***** ******* ****!

**** **** *************** *****!

*** *****!

There isn't any point writing the actual words. They were mostly all the same and really VERY boring. Especially when you've heard them as often as I have.

I mean, they just *do* it all the time. After a bit I shouted, at the top of my voice: "Just SHUT UP, I'm SICK OF IT!"

So then they both spun round to look at me, like, "Who's this telling us to shut up? Where has she  come from?" And then they remembered that I lived there, and that I was their daughter – well, supposedly – and the Vampire said, "You should've rung me! Why didn't you ring me?"

"Didn't think you'd be interested," I said.

She didn't like it when I said that. She did this flinching thing, like I'd made the sign of the cross or breathed garlic over her.

"Well, of course I'd have been interested!"

Dunno why. She wasn't interested before, when she was away doing something and I rang to ask what I was supposed to have for supper. She got quite stroppy and said, "Oh, for goodness' sake! Can't I even go away for one night? Just look in the fridge and help yourself!" In other words, LEAVE ME ALONE. I don't want to be PESTERED.

I didn't bother reminding her. I mean, really, why bother?

"I thought you'd be too busy," I said.

The Vampire said well, yes, she had been busy. "But you could've always rung your dad."

I told her that I'd tried. "He didn't answer."

At this the Vampire narrowed her eyes and breathed very deeply and said, "I see!" To which the Invisible Man immediately barked, "See what?"

"That you obviously had no desire to be contacted!" snarled the Vampire. "I wonder why not?"

Which set them off, all over again. I just left them to it. They're as bad as each other and it drives me nuts. I wouldn't care if they both went off and never came back. I can manage on my own. I've proved that! Course, I'd need some money, but there's plenty of stuff here I could flog. Either that, or you know what. Well, I know what! Anyone else that might be reading this, ON PAIN OF DEATH, won't have the least idea what I'm talking about. Which is fine by me! I don't intend to spell it out. There's ways; that's all I'm gonna say. I WOULD NOT GO HUNGRY! You have to look out for yourself in this world and that's what I aim to do. Gotta be prepared. I've been preparing since I was nine years old. No way am I just gonna sit in my bedroom and cry. Not again. Not ever.

They're still at it, down there. Still carrying on. Probably one day they'll split up and then they'll be quarrelling over which one's gotta be responsible for me. SHE won't wanna be, HE won't wanna be.

WHO CARES???

Went round to Spice's on Saturday for tea. We had all stuff that the Vampire won't buy. Crisps and cakes and sticky puds. Pretty cool! The Vampire says it's junk food and will make you F.A.T. She's more terrified of F.A.T than anything else. I bet she'd sooner have a brain tumour than suffer F.A.T. I'm gonna buy her a trick tape measure for her birthday, so when she measures herself, like she does practically every week, she'll think her waist's expanded by about five centimetres and then won't she SHRIEEEEEK!

I reckon a bit of junk food would do her good – she looks like one of those wire coat hangers with clothes hung on it. I think I'm gonna start eating junk food. I'm gonna get as fat as fat can be, so fat I can't move. I'll just, like, lie there, in a big jellified heap on the floor, and she'll keep tripping over me, until in the end she has to stop and look, and see what it is, and she'll discover that it's ME. Her DAUGHTER. Shock horror! The shame of it. That'll show her!

It was OK round Spice's. Don't think her mum likes me too much, but so what? I'm used to it. In any case, who needs to be liked? Not me! I can't stand people that creep and crawl and are willing to do just ANYTHING to gain approval.

Spice's little brother is quite cute. I guess I wouldn't mind having a brother. I wouldn't want a sister. NO THANK YOU! But a brother would be neat, so long as he was little, and then when the Vampire went off and the Invisible Man disappeared we'd be left by ourselves and I'd look out for him, see he was all right. I wouldn't ever let him go hungry, or be frightened. He'd know there was nothing to worry about so long as I was there. But fat chance of the Vampire ever having another kid! She made one BIG MISTAKE having me – she's not likely to do it again.

Dunno how Spice manages, though, not having her own space. Drive me bonkers that would. People around me all the time. Just ONE person's all I'd want. But not the Vampire or the Invisible Man. Gotta be someone that really wants me.

Yeah! SOME HOPE.

six

On Monday, at school, Shay said to me, "Now that I've been round your place, I s'ppose you'd better come round mine."

I was quite shocked! I was really surprised that she'd want to see me out of school. It had to mean she looked on me as a real proper friend. After all, you don't invite just anyone back. It has to be someone you like.

"What d'you reckon?" She was looking at me in that way that she did, like really *piercing*. If you were someone she didn't rate, like one of the mindless blobs, it could practically shrivel you on the spot. "This Saturday? Wanna come?"

I beamed and nodded and said, "Yes, please!"

"Won't be anything special," said Shay. "Not like round your place."

She really thought my place was *special*?

"All that stuff your mum got in... won't be anything like that."

"Oh! Well, you know, she gets it from work." It wasn't any secret, now, that Mum worked in Tesco's.

"Think she'd get you some garlic?" said Shay.

I said, "*Garlic?* What'd I want garlic for?"

"Protect yourself. Told you my mum was a vampire, didn't I?"

I thought this was meant to be funny, so I laughed and waited for Shay to laugh, too. Instead, very solemnly, she said, "Best come

prepared... don't s'ppose you've got a crucifix by any chance?"

Bewildered, I said, "N-no."

"Looks like it'll have to be the garlic, then... they don't like garlic.

Garlic and crucifixes. They're the only protection –
apart from a stake through the heart."

I swallowed; I was getting a bit nervous. Not that I
really thought Shay's mum was a vampire, of course I
didn't! There aren't such things as vampires. But what
sort of woman was she?

"Oh, don't worry," said Shay. "She won't get you.
Doesn't usually come out of her coffin till about five
o'clock. But you'd better bring some garlic, just in
case!"

Shay had this really wicked sense of humour. Like
really ghoulish. The only trouble was I couldn't always
be sure when she was joking and when she was being
serious. Sometimes it seemed like she was being both
together.

Anyway, I said that I'd love to go round, and we
agreed that we'd meet up at three o'clock in the
shopping centre, on Saturday afternoon, and I'd go back
with her. When I asked Mum, that evening, if it would
be all right, Mum said, "Oh! Visiting the nobs, are we?"

I didn't understand what she was talking about. I
thought she meant *knobs*, like door knobs. Apparently
she meant "nobs" as in posh people.

"Dunno what you're going to wear," said Mum. "I
can't afford to buy you new clothes."

I said, "Why can't I wear what I always wear?"

"Doesn't look like you've got much choice."

She'd noticed that when Shay came to visit, her clothes had been what Mum called "quality". I hadn't noticed cos I don't think I've got much fashion sense, but Mum has an eye for these things. She said Shay's gear was "all designer labels... ridiculous on a girl her age!" To me it had just been a black jacket and black jeans and black boots. Everything black!

"Yes, and everything costing a bomb," said Mum. "Take it from me, she didn't pick that lot up from British Home Stores. Well, I'm sorry! We just can't afford to compete."

I didn't want to compete. I knew that I couldn't, anyway; not with Shay. But Mum had gone and made me self-conscious, so that I looked at my clothes in the wardrobe, which I had to share with the Terrible Two, and for the first time thought how horrible and shabby they were. What had I worn last Saturday, when Shay came? A shapeless old coat that had once been quilted and was now sagging and flat. And *grey*. And *torn*.

Boring blue joggers, all thin and baggy from too much washing. Ancient trainers, which had never been new in the first place. Well, they obviously had for someone, but not for me. We'd got them at a jumble sale in the church hall, which is where we get most of our clothes. It had never bothered me before, but suddenly I wanted designer labels, like Shay. Or if not designer labels, at least things that were *new*, and which I'd been able to choose for myself. Not all this stinky old stuff that had been worn by other people!

In spite of what she'd said, Mum was obviously anxious for me to make a good impression cos she came home the very next evening with a brand new top that she'd got from Tesco's.

"I thought it would go quite well with your tartan skirt."

Mum was right – it did. I just wished that I could be more grateful, cos I knew that money didn't grow on trees and we had to count every penny, and the Terrible Two needed new shoes, and Mum and Dad hadn't had a holiday in simply years, but oh, I'd have so loved to have had a new skirt as well! *And* to have chosen for myself.

Mum must have sensed that I wasn't as enthusiastic as I should have been, cos quite sharply she said, "Well,

I'm sorry, it's the best I can do. If you will choose friends that are out of your league..."

But I hadn't! I hadn't chosen Shay any more than I'd chosen my new top. Shay was the one who'd done the choosing. I said this to Mum, who said, "I can't imagine what she picked on you for. You've got nothing in common! What have you got in common?"

That was something that had puzzled me. Shay was so sure of herself, so up-front, so... well! Independent. I was just plain ordinary Ruth, who wouldn't say boo to a beetle. Why had she chosen *me*?

I didn't know, but I was very glad that she had. Things were so much better, now that Shay was looking out for me. Nobody bullied me and nobody bothered me. I almost, even, quite enjoyed going to school, which meant Mum didn't have to bellow and bawl at me every morning to get out of bed. Karina was still a bit of a problem as Amie Phillips didn't seem to want anything to do with her and I felt bad when I saw her hanging out by herself, so that sometimes, when Shay wasn't around, I tried talking to her. But I always ended up wishing that I hadn't as she was so nasty and said such hateful things. Like one day it was, "I see she's still got you in her clutches, then," and another day, "Did she give you her *permission*?"

When she said that I got cross and snapped, "I don't need permission! I can talk to whoever I like."

Karina, looking sly, said, "Oh, yeah?"

I said, "Yeah!" And it was true. I didn't need Shay's permission to talk to her. I only waited till Shay wasn't around cos I wanted to avoid unpleasantness. For Karina's sake. I did it for Karina! But I was fast coming to the conclusion that it wasn't worth it. I mean, I was going out of my way to be polite and friendly and she was just, like, sneering at me all the time. I decided that I wouldn't bother any more.

On Saturday, when I set off to meet Shay in my nice new Tesco top – covered up, alas, by the same old tatty coat – Mum said, "How are you going to get back? I don't want you crossing town by yourself in the dark!"

I'd been wondering about this, but I didn't want Mum getting fussed and suddenly telling me I couldn't go, so I brightly said that Shay's mum or dad would bring me back and scooted off, quickly, towards the lift before Mum could ask any more awkward questions.

Shay was waiting for me in the shopping centre, perched on the rim of one of the big flower tubs outside WHSmith. She was wearing her black outfit again and this time I looked more closely and I saw that Mum was right, it was dead classy! And it really suited her. Mum, being a bit sniffy, had said that black was "no colour for a young girl", but it wasn't *all* black, cos the trousers had little flared bits with bright red flowers, and the top had red piping all round it, and in any case Shay didn't look like a young girl, she looked more like about fifteen. She made me feel really babyish.

"Get a load of this," she said, holding out a carrier bag. "I've been round the stores, getting stuff for our tea. What d'you reckon?"

I took one look in the bag and went, "Wow!"

"Is it enough?"

"That'd feed an army," I said.

It looked like she'd visited every food shop in the centre. There was stuff from Sainsbury's, stuff from  Marks, stuff from the cake shop in the Arcade, stuff from the chocolate shop on the top level, even stuff from the health food shop.

"Yeah, I dunno about that," said Shay. "I'm actually getting into junk food right now. It's just they had this lying about, so I took some. Oh, and look! I got this for you." She thrust her hand into the bag and pulled something out. Garlic! "Remember, if the Vampire appears, just hold it up, like this, then she can't get you."

I giggled, but a bit uncertainly. I said, "That's a joke, right?"

"Best not take any chances," said Shay.

We caught the bus to Shay's place. She lived up on the hill, just out of town, in an actual real house with its own grass outside, and a proper bit of garden at the back.

Shay said, "Stupid if you ask me! Why can't we all live in flats? Wouldn't take up nearly as much space."

I expect that is true, but I don't care! I have decided that when I am grown up and can afford it, that is when I am a doctor – if I get to pass my exams – I am going to have a house *just like Shay's*. Shay said, "It's not anything special. There's houses heaps bigger than this. This is just a titchy little thing."

Well! It may have seemed titchy to her, but I could hardly believe it. It had three floors, with different sorts of rooms on each floor, like a special room for watching

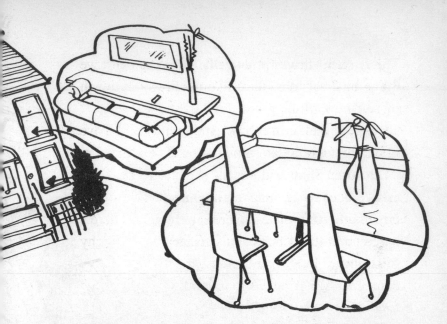

television in and a special room for eating in and a
basement where the kitchen was. Shay said we'd go
down to the kitchen first of all and dump our junk food
ready for later. The way she said it, "our junk food", she
made it sound like it was some sort of gormy dish that
you might get in a restaurant. Except that I don't think
it's spelt gormy, cos I think it's French. I think it might
be *gourmet*.

"Bacon-flavoured crisps," said Shay, lovingly.
"Chocolate-covered jelly babies... fudge ice cream.
This is going to be good!"

She led the way down some steps and into this huge
great room like an underground cavern. There was a
long counter running down the middle and rows of pots
and pans, and strings of onions hanging off the walls.

The kitchen! It was practically as big as the whole of our flat. I thought to myself how Mum would love it; she's always complaining how she can't move for tripping over bodies.

"Right." Shay laid out all her bits and pieces, her bacon-flavoured crisps and chocolate-covered jelly babies, and sticky buns and sausage rolls, in a long line across the counter. "We'll leave our junk food *here*," she said, moving a potted plant out of the way. "And now we'll go up to my room."

Shay's room was on the top floor. All the time we're going up the stairs I'm, like, looking over my shoulder in case her mum, the Vampire, might suddenly appear.

"It's OK," said Shay. "I told you, she hardly ever gets out of her coffin till five o'clock. They shrivel in the light, vampires do."

I whispered, "W-where is her coffin?"

Shay cackled and said, "In there!" pointing at a room on the second floor. "Better tiptoe or she might wake up and come and sink her fangs into us!"

I scurried like a frightened mouse up the last flight of stairs. As I scurried I couldn't help noticing how neat and clean everything was. At home we live in a state of what Mum calls "clutter". There's toys everywhere, clothes everywhere. Stuff waiting to be ironed, stuff waiting to be put away. Shoes. Socks. Dad's breakfast tray. It just all mounts up. Plus there's a big stain on the carpet where I tripped over with a bowl of soup (which I was taking in to Dad), and another, smaller stain where Sammy dropped his bread and jam and then went and trod it in, not to mention marks on the wall made by grubby fingers (mainly those belonging to the Terrible Two) and this thick oily dust, all black and treacly, that leaks in from outside and is very bad, Mum says, for Dad's emphysema and Lisa's chest. (It's why she snuffles all the time.)

There wasn't any black dust in Shay's house. There wasn't any dust at all. No stains on the carpet, no marks on the wall. No shoes or socks or piles of clothes. It was just *sooo* beautiful! It's how I shall keep my house, when I have one. It's how I *try* to keep my bit of bedroom, but without very much success, cos it's impossible to stop Kez and Lisa from trespassing.

As we reached the top landing, I hissed, "How does your mum keep it all so nice?"

I felt really ashamed when I compared what Shay's place was like with how it was at home. I didn't blame Mum for all the mess; I knew she didn't have time to keep dusting and cleaning and tidying up. But I still felt ashamed, and wondered what Shay must have thought.

"Do you help?" I said.

Shay said no. "Mrs Kelly does it."

I said, "Who's Mrs Kelly?"

"Person that comes in and cleans," said Shay. "Quick!" She grabbed me and pushed me ahead of her through the door. "Before the Vampire gets wind of us!"

I was quite astonished at the state of Shay's room. On the door there was this big angry notice: **PRIVATE. KEEP OUT. THIS MEANS YOU.** But I didn't think there was any need to have a notice; just one quick look would be enough to frighten people off. It was like a tip! It was even worse than my bit of bedroom when the Terrible Two had been on the rampage. It looked like someone had emptied bin bags full of rubbish in there. Totally *in-de-SCRIBABLE*. But if I had to – describe it, I mean – I'd say:

Tops, bottoms, shoes, socks, knickers

Coke bottles, water bottles, sweet wrappers

Knives, forks, spoons

Books, bags, papers

Pens, pencils

Magazines

CDs

And just general *junk*.

Loads of it, absolutely everywhere.

"You coming in, or what?" said Shay.

I slithered past a saucepan containing the shrivelled remains of what looked like spaghetti and waded across the floor through a sea of clothes.

"Don't worry about that lot." Shay kicked them, contemptuously, out of the way. "Sit down!"

I stared round, helplessly. Sit down where??? Every available bit of space was covered.

"Here!" Shay swept a hand across the bed and a pile of papers went flying up into the air like a flock of pigeons, then slowly settled back down again, all out of order. If, that is, they'd ever been in any order. Mine always are, but that's because I hate not being able to find stuff. It upset me, seeing so much mess and muddle.

"How do you know where anything is?" I said.

Shay said, "Don't wanna know where anything is."

"But how do you *find* things?"

"Don't wanna find things. If I wanna find things—" she stuck her toe in the middle of the papers and stirred them up again, "I put 'em somewhere. All this is just muck."

It *was* muck. I didn't know how she could live like that!

"I thought you said your mum had someone that came and did the cleaning?"

"Mrs Kelly. Yeah."

"So why doesn't she come and do your room?"

"Cos she's not allowed. No one's allowed. Not without permission." Shay marched over and yanked open the door. She jabbed a finger at the angry notice. "See? See what it says? **PRIVATE! KEEP OUT!**"

"Even your mum?" I said.

"My mum? What'd she wanna come in for?"

"Well... I don't know! Put clothes away? My mum's always coming into our room."

"Your mum's different," said Shay.

Or maybe, I thought, it was Shay's mum that was different. My mum was normal! Most people's mums went into their bedrooms. Millie's mum did. Mariam's mum did. Whoever heard of a mum being told to keep out?

"Wanna hear some music?" said Shay. She picked a CD off the floor. "What sorta music d'you like?"

"Um... anything, really," I said.

Shay unearthed a CD player from beneath a pile of clothes and slid the disc in. A weird wailing and banging filled the room.

"Yay! Freaky!" Shay jumped on to the bed, and off again. "That's cool! That's my kind of sound!"

It was pretty loud.

"Won't it wake your mum?" I said, nervously.

"Who cares?" Shay danced about the room, trampling on all the litter, some of which went *crack!* or *scrunch!* beneath her feet. I thought, this is gross! I was just so surprised at Shay, of all people.

"Ooh! Look at you!" Shay skipped round me, laughing and scrunching. "You look like a prune!" And she sucked in her cheeks so that her lips practically disappeared inside her mouth, which made me feel that I was being sour and small-minded. I was glad I hadn't admitted to her that last Christmas I'd actually asked  Mum and Dad if I could have a filing cabinet, one of those metal ones with drawers, *and a key*, so that I could put all my things away nicely in different-coloured files, with proper labels, in alphabetical order, so Kez and Lisa couldn't get at them. I had this feeling that she'd utterly despise me. (I didn't get the filing cabinet, anyway; Mum said they were too expensive and that in any case there wasn't any room.)

"Wanna see what I keep in here?" said Shay. She pulled open a drawer, where normally, I should think, people would put knickers and socks and pairs of tights, and dumped the contents on the bed beside me. I gasped; I couldn't help it. It was full of jewellery!

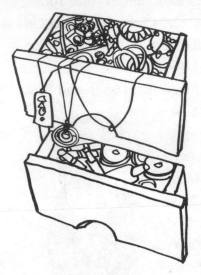

Bracelets and chains, rings, necklaces, hair slides, all winking and glittering.

"And in *here*—" she yanked out a second drawer, "I got make-up."

I could feel my eyes boggling. I had never seen so many pots and tubs and tubes and jars.

"I call it my collection," said Shay.

I remembered what she'd said about her mum being a beauty consultant. I thought perhaps that was where she'd got it from, but scornfully she said, "Nah! Got it myself, didn't I? There's loads of other stuff I could show you. I got—"

And then she stopped, and I felt this little shiver run through me. Someone was calling up the stairs.

"Shay!"

Could it be the Vampire?

Shay ran out on to the landing. "What d'you want?"

"I wanted t— Oh! Hallo. Who's this?"

Curiosity had made me a little bit brave. I'd gone pattering out behind Shay. I just couldn't resist! Shay scowled and said, "Someone from school."

"And doesn't someone from school have a name?"

I squeaked, "I'm Ruth Spicer."

"Well, hallo there, Ruth Spicer! I'm Shay's mum."

I could see why Shay called her the Vampire. Unlike Shay, who was dark-skinned, her mum was very pale, like a water lily. She just had no colour at all, and was so amazingly slender that she looked like the long white stem of a plant. She'd made up her eyes with thick black stuff on the lashes and purple on the eyelids, while her mouth and fingernails were deep blood red. I wasn't sure that I'd like her for a mum, but she was kind of fascinating, in a weird sort of way.

"Are you staying for tea?" she said.

"Yes, she is," said Shay. "I've got all the stuff."

"I saw." The Vampire tightened her blood red lips. She was obviously not pleased about something, but whether it was me staying to tea, or Shay not telling her that I was staying to tea, or something else entirely, I couldn't quite work out. "I presume," she said, "that that was what you wanted?"

"What?" said Shay.

"For me to see!"

"Dunno what you're talking about."

"Oh, come on! Everything all nicely laid out so I couldn't miss it?"

"I just laid it out ready," said Shay.

Slowly, her mum shook her head. "You do these things on purpose, don't you? Your one aim in life is to rile me. Well, all right! Go ahead, stuff yourself with artificial muck. Why should I bother?"

"You shouldn't," said Shay.

"No, well, I'm not going to. I'm off down the gym, now, then I'm meeting up with Boo and Ellie. I probably won't be back till late, but your father should be here well before then. He said he'd be home by eight. OK? Nice to meet you, Ruth. Have fun!"

"She really *hates* me eating junk food," said Shay, as we returned to her bedroom. "It drives her whacko!" She sounded quite jubilant about it, so that I began to think maybe her mum was right, and it really was her aim in life. "You don't have to look like that, prune face! She already is a whacko. Can't you tell?" She made her eyes go crossed and stuck out her tongue and waggled her fingers either side of her head. "Totally bonkers! Wanna try on some of my jewellery?"

I hesitated. I was worried by the thought of her dad not getting home till eight o'clock, because Mum was expecting me ages before then. I said apologetically to Shay that maybe I'd better leave now, while it was still light.

"I know it's silly," I said, though I didn't really think it was, "but my mum gets all fussed if I'm out late on my own."

"Won't be on your own," said Shay. "I'll come with you."

"But how will you get back?"

"Same as I did last week. Told you the Vampire wasn't the worrying sort. She doesn't care what I do – apart from eating junk food!"

I was beginning to think that Shay lived in a very peculiar sort of family. I couldn't imagine my mum and dad not caring what I did. *Or* going out and leaving me in the flat by myself. I'm always wishing that I could have a room of my own and enjoy a bit of peace and quiet, but I'd absolutely hate it if the whole flat was empty. I think, actually, I'd be a bit scared. Shay obviously wasn't scared, but maybe that was because she was used to it. It just didn't seem to bother her.

After we'd tried on some of her jewellery, and listened to another CD that she discovered by almost treading on it, we went down to the kitchen to eat our junk food. I suppose it was junk food. Shay said it was, though it seemed just ordinary to me. When we'd finished eating, I said that I'd have to go or Mum would start frothing, so Shay came with me all the way across town. I did feel a bit guilty seeing her go off again by herself, and thought that if anything happened to her it would be all my fault, but she really didn't seem to mind.

Mum opened the front door. She said, "Ah, there you are! Not before time. Did they bring you back?"

I said yes, because after all Shay *had* brought me back, and Mum then said, "I hope they saw you up in the lift?" to which I made a fluffy sort of mumbling sound.

"I hope they did!" said Mum, following me into the kitchen. "That lift's not safe this time of night – anyone could get in there with you. So what was it like? What's her mum like?"

I wasn't going to say that Shay's mum was a vampire and a whacko. I had more sense than that! I said, "She's very thin – she looks like a model." Mum sniffed and said that she could probably afford to.

"I suppose the place is dead posh?"

"Yes, but it's not as cosy as ours."

I said it partly cos I knew that it would please Mum, and partly cos it was true. Shay's place wasn't cosy, any more than Shay herself was. But I still felt flattered that she'd invited me!

seven

The next week was half term. I didn't think, probably, that Shay would want to bother seeing me at half term, so when Millie called round and asked if I'd like to sleep over her place one night, I was quite pleased.

It was ages since Millie and I had done anything together. I could tell that Mum was pleased, too. She likes Millie and I don't think, really, that she did like Shay. She always said that she was "too knowing". I've never actually understood this, as I wouldn't have thought it would be possible to be *too* knowing. I'd have thought the more you knew, the better. But Mum obviously felt it was a bad thing, maybe because she thought Shay knew things she ought not to know, like grown-up type things, whereas Millie (Mum said) was "natural and unspoilt". I dunno! Just because Millie lived round the corner and wore the sort of clothes that Mum considered "suitable". She didn't consider Shay's clothes suitable. It really irritated her, Shay going round in designer labels. She kept on and on about it.

"Totally ridiculous! A girl that age."

So when I asked if it was OK for me to spend the night with Millie she said yes without any hesitation, even though she'd been hinting that it would be nice, now it was half term, if I could stay in and keep an eye on the kids for a change, while she went out. Dad would still have been there, cos Dad hasn't left the flat for I don't know how long, but Mum would never leave him on his own all evening with Sammy and the Terrible Two. I knew she'd been looking forward to having some time off and I thought perhaps I was being selfish, wanting to go to Millie's. But Mum seemed really keen.

"Maybe you'll get back together again. I'd far rather you had Millie as a friend than that Shay."

It was fun, being round at Millie's. For a little while it was almost like we were back at Juniors again, giggling together and sharing secrets. But Mariam had been with us then; it didn't seem the same without her.

It had always been the three of us. Millie said she'd called round Mariam's place and hadn't been able to get any reply.

"Someone said they'd moved."

I said, "*All* of them?"

"It's what they said."

"I thought it was just Mariam! So she could go to another school."

"I'm just telling you what I was told," said Millie.

I twizzled my toes under the duvet. (We were lying in bed at the time.) "Wish I could go to another school! Don't you? Wouldn't you like to go somewhere else? If you could choose."

"Dunno." Millie shrugged. "Krapfilled's OK."

"I think it's horrible," I said.

"That's cos you don't join in."

"Nobody ever asks me!" I said.

"So whose fault's that?" Millie rolled over to look at me. She propped herself on an elbow. "You go round making like you're so *supeeeeeerior*—"

I was indignant. "I do not!"

"You do. You just don't realise you're doing it."

I couldn't think what to say to that. I muttered that I didn't *feel* superior.

"It's the way you come across," said Millie. "Specially now you're hanging out with that Shayanne Sugar. She's really freaky!"

"She's my friend," I said.

"Yeah? Sooner you than me!"

Growing desperate, I said, "I only started going round with Shay cos there wasn't anyone else. Cos you and Mariam were both in gangs. I'd heaps rather you and me could still be friends!"

"We can be," said Millie. "Out of school."

"Why not in school?"

"You know why not in school!"

"Because of *gangs*," I said. "I hate gangs! I just hate them!"

"Well, there you go," said Millie.

I knew, then, that me and Millie could never get back together again. We could never be proper best friends.

"Gangs make people stupid," I said. "They make people do things they don't want to do. They make them all *follow my leader*. I couldn't ever belong to a gang!"

"You know your trouble?" said Millie. "You just don't try. You go to a new place, you gotta learn to fit in. Otherwise you'll just be, like, an outsider all the time."

It's what I was: an outsider. But at least I had Shay!

"How about we meet up again tomorrow?" said Millie, as she walked back with me through the estate the next day. "I'll call round... eleven o'clock. We'll do something. OK?"

I said OK, thinking that even just seeing her out of school was better than not seeing her at all, but then, quite suddenly, the following morning when I was least expecting it, I got this phone call from Shay.

"Hi, Spice! What you up to?"

I said, "Nothing very much."

"Me neither. Wanna meet? Shopping centre, same place as before? See you in half an hour. Don't be late!"

I forgot all about Millie. I said to Dad that I was going to meet someone in the shopping centre, and was about to go whizzing off when the Terrible Two started up, wanting to come with me. I told them that they couldn't.

"I'm meeting a friend."

"You're meeting *her*! You're meeting that girl!"

I said, "What *girl*?"

"That Shay person!"

I said, "So what if I am?"

"Mum doesn't like you seeing her," said Lisa, all virtuous.

"No, an' you're s'pposed to be looking after us," whined Kez.

"You never take us anywhere!"

"Who'd want to?" I said. I slammed the front door behind me and scooted off to the lift before Dad could find enough breath to tell me I couldn't go.

It wasn't till I got off the bus at the shopping centre and saw the hands of the big clock pointing to eleven that I remembered... Millie was supposed to be calling round! For just a moment I felt a pang of guilt, but then I reminded myself that Millie wasn't really, properly, my friend any more. When we were in school she hardly ever spoke to me. What kind of friend was that? Shay was the one who was my friend. She was the one who looked out for me and made it OK for me to do my homework and not get bullied or picked on if it was read out in class. I didn't care any more about Millie. She didn't stick up for me. Let her go round with her stupid gang, if that was what she wanted.

On my way in to the centre I passed a girl from school. Varya. She was with her mum – well, I suppose it was her mum. She smiled at me and said hallo, and I said hallo back, and as I did so I suddenly realised that it was the *very first time* I'd ever spoken to her. She mostly kept to herself and for some reason nobody ever bothered her. I'd always thought she seemed quite an interesting sort of person, but she didn't speak very much English and I was too shy to go and talk to her because how would we manage to communicate? But that day in the shopping centre she was, like, really friendly, like really pleased to see me, and her mum was, too, smiling and nodding as we passed, so that I went on my way feeling quite bubbly.

Shay was already there and waiting for me. I broke into a trot when I saw her.

"Sorry I'm late!"

"You're not late. I was early. *She* brought me."

"The Va—" Hastily, I corrected myself. "Your mum?"

"*The Vampire.* Yeah! She dropped me off. What shall we do? Wanna go and mooch round Sander's?"

Sander's is this big department store, which is brilliant for mooching as parts of it are like street markets with racks and racks of clothes, and one entire floor which is called The Bazaar, where you can find just about anything you could ever dream of. Shay said, "Let's go to Jewellery." She led the way and I followed. Sander's is *so* enormous that left to myself I would most probably panic and get lost, but Shay obviously knew her way around.

"Jewellery's my favourite," she said. "This is where I always come."

It's really beautiful in the jewellery department. There's counter after counter, piled high, everything all winking and flashing in a thousand different colours, like an Aladdin's cave. We wandered round, touching things and picking things up and trying on bracelets and chains. Shay found some earrings that she fancied. They were in the shape of parrots, swinging on a perch: bright red and blue and emerald green. They would've looked stupid on me as I have this rather ridiculous face, very small and squashed, but on Shay I could see they would be totally brilliant. I urged her to get them, and she was obviously tempted. She held them up by her ears and said, "What d'you reckon?"

"I think you should buy them," I said.

"Mm... dunno! I'll think about it." She put the parrots back and reached out for something else. "Hey, look! These would suit you!"

She'd found some tiny little earrings in the shape of flowers. I agreed that they were sweet, but I couldn't imagine ever wearing them.

"So what would you get," said Shay, "if you were going to get something?"

What I'd always, always wanted was a silver chain. I said this to Shay and she cried, "Let's look!"

There were so many silver chains that it was really difficult to decide which one I should go for, but in the end I settled on one which had a tiny little pixie figure hanging from it.

"That's Cornish, that is," said Shay. "Cornish pixie. That's a good luck charm! Is that what you'd get?"

I said yes, but of course I couldn't get it as I didn't have any money. But it was fun just looking. I mean, it didn't make me discontented or anything.

After we'd done a bit more mooching, Shay said we should go up to the self-service and get something to eat and drink. I quickly said that I wasn't hungry, but Shay said, "That's all right, I'll pay for it." Like she knew I didn't have any money and wanted to spare me the embarrassment of being forced to admit it. I didn't argue, cos it would've been rude when she'd made the offer. She bought us a Coke each, and a packet of crisps, and gave the lady at the till a five pound note. The lady asked if she had "the odd 2p" but Shay said she hadn't.

"See?" She opened her purse and shook it upside down. "This is all I've got."

I said, "I can give you 2p," feeling glad that I could make a contribution, even just a small one.

"I've got loads more money at home," said Shay. "I've got money in the building society. I can take it out whenever I want. It's just that I don't bring much with me cos of muggers."

I giggled at that. I couldn't imagine anyone being bold enough to mug Shay!

"Just let anyone try it," she said. "I'd bash 'em to a pulp! But I don't need the hassle, you know?"

After our crisps and Coke we went back out into the shopping centre and mooched round a few more shops, until Shay suddenly stopped and said there was something she'd got to do.

"Just wait there." She pointed at a seat, and I obediently sat down. "I'll only be a few minutes. Don't move! OK?"

I said OK. I didn't mind sitting there, watching people walk past, though I did wonder where Shay had rushed off to in such a hurry, and what she was going to do. She'd only been gone about two seconds when a girl came up to me and said, "Was that Shay Sugar I saw you with?"

I said yes, and she scrunched up her face into an expression of... well! Like if you saw a scorpion scuttling across the pavement. *Look out there's a scorpion* kind of thing.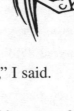

"D'you know her?" I said.

"She used to go to my school."

"Oh. She goes to my school now," I said.

"Is she a friend of yours?"

I nodded. The girl went, "Hm!" I began to feel a bit uneasy; this girl didn't seem to care for Shay very much. "I'd watch out, if I were you," she said.

"Why?" I crinkled my nose, which I happen to know  (cos I've done it in front of a mirror) looks really silly, but I can't seem to help it. It's a *mannerism*. "Why have I got to watch out?"

"I just would, that's all."

My nose went crinkle, crinkle again. I can actually, sometimes, be quite stubborn. According to Mum I can. I said, "But *why*?"

"Cos she'll make you do things."

"What things?"

"Things you don't want to do."

"I don't do anything I don't want to do!"

"That's what you think," said the girl.

I wondered why she was saying this to me. She didn't look like the sort of person who would spread malicious gossip. What I mean is, she was blonde and prettyish and had blue eyes. People with blue eyes always look like they're soft and gentle. But of course you never can tell. Looks can be deceiving.

Shay came back at that moment. She and the girl looked at each other, and both together they said, "Hi!"

"How's your new school?" said the girl.

"OK. How's St Margaret's?"

"A lot quieter without you there."

"Everywhere's a lot quieter without me," said Shay. "Must be *sooo* boring."

"Some people like it that way."

"Yeah? Some people are just mindless blobs."

"That's your opinion," said the girl.

"Course it is! Wouldn't quote anyone else's, would I?"

The girl said, "Who knows?"

"I do," said Shay.

So then the girl, like, gave up. She just went "Huh!" and stalked off in what I think is called a dudgeon, though I'm not actually sure what a dudgeon is.

It's indignation! I just looked it up. I think it's a good word and I'm going to start using it. *Dudgeon.*

"She's so stupid, that girl," said Shay. She put her arm round my waist, in a companionable fashion. "I'll walk you to the bus stop."

When I got home, Mum was there as it was her afternoon off. She was looking like a big black thundercloud. What had I done now???

"Where have you been?" she said.

"In the shopping centre."

"For *four solid hours*?"

"Dad knew where I was! I told him."

"And what about Millie? Did you tell Millie? You didn't, did you?" I shook my head. "Ruth, it's not good enough! You can't let people down like this."

"I'm sorry," I mumbled. "I forgot."

"That's no excuse! How do you think she felt, turning up on the doorstep and Lisa telling her you'd gone out? I suppose you were with that Shay?"

"She's my friend," I said.

"So's Millie – and she's been your friend for far longer!"

I protested that Millie wasn't properly my friend. Not any more.

"Why not?" said Mum.

"I told you," I said. "She's in this gang. She doesn't even talk to me when we're at school. If it wasn't for Shay, nobody would talk to me!"

"Why aren't you in a gang?" said Lisa.

"Cos I don't want to be!"

"I would. I'd be in the *best* gang. I—"

"Oh, shut up!" I said. I took off my coat and slung it over the back of a chair. As I did so, something fell out of the pocket. Something shiny. Lisa immediately pounced.

"What's this?"

"Yes, what it is it?" said Mum.

Lisa squealed, and held it up. "Ooh, pretty!"

It was the silver chain I'd picked out. How had it got in my pocket?

"Where did you get that from?" said Mum.

Quickly, I said, "Shay gave it to me."

She must have done; it was the only explanation. She

must have rushed off to the building society to take some money out, cos I knew she didn't have any more on her, then rushed back into Sander's and bought the chain. Then she must have slipped it in my pocket when I wasn't looking. It must have been when she put her arm round me. I'd thought at the time that it was an unusual thing for Shay to do. We didn't have a touchy-feely sort of relationship at all; not like I'd had with Millie. Me and Millie were always going round with our arms linked. Mum used to laugh at us and say it was like we were joined at the hip. But with Shay it had felt a bit uncomfortable, to tell the truth. Why couldn't she just have said, straight out, "I've bought you something?" Maybe she'd though I wouldn't take it off her.

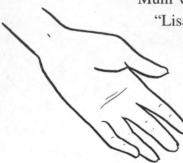

Mum was holding out her hand. "Lisa, let me have a look at that. Are you telling me, that Shay actually bought this for you?"

I said yes. I mean, how else could it have got there? I hadn't taken it!

"It's a Cornish pixie," I said. "It's a good luck charm."

"Hm…" Mum was examining it, closely. "Well, it's not top quality. It can't have cost that much. All the same—" She handed it back to me. "She really shouldn't be buying you things."

"It's all right," I said. "She's got loads of money! She's got a *building society* account."

"Oh, I'm sure she has," said Mum. "But in future, just say no. OK? You don't have to be rude about it, just say your mum doesn't want you accepting things. And, Ruth—" She crooked a finger at me. "Just pick up that telephone and call Millie. I want to hear you apologise."

eight

When we went back to school after half term, I told Shay thank you for my chain. Shay said, "You've got to wear it all the time, it'll bring you good luck."

"I can't wear it to school," I said, shocked. The very thought! Wearing my precious chain to Krapfilled High!

"I'd wear my earrings," said Shay, "except they'd probably make me take them off."

"You got them?" I said. "You got your earrings?"

"Thought I might as well. Seemed silly not to. But I don't reckon they'd let me go round with parrots in my ears... don't s'ppose they'd mind a chain, though."

"But someone might steal it!"

"Not with me around."

"No, it's too beautiful," I said. "It's the most beautiful thing I've ever had and I shall cherish it always. But Mum—" I added this bit reluctantly. "Mum says you mustn't go spending your money on me."

Shay gave one of her cackles of laughter. "Tell your mum she doesn't have to worry!"

"She really means it. I don't think she'd let me take anything else. She nearly made me give my chain back."

"That'd be daft. What'd she wanna do that for?"

I shook my head. I sort of understood how Mum felt, but I didn't want to say anything that might sound ungracious.

"It's what being friends is all about," said Shay. "I don't see why I can't give you stuff if I want."

"Cos I can't give you stuff," I said. "I haven't got anything!"

Shay said what did that matter? "It's not important!"

"It is to me," I said. "I'd like to give you something."

"Yeah?" She considered me a moment, through narrowed eyes, like she was trying to decide whether I was serious. "Maybe, in that case..."

"What?"

"We'll see what we can do."

She wouldn't say any more, so I was left not knowing what she meant. I kept trying to think of anything at all I might have that Shay would like, but I couldn't. All my stuff was old, and chipped, and tatty. Most of it had come from jumble sales. The only really valuable object I possessed was my silver chain. *Silvery* chain. I knew it wasn't real silver, but it was still my most treasured possession.

I now went round with Shay all the time at school. It was just something that seemed to have happened. Karina had drifted away, and hardly ever spoke to me. Millie never had spoken much, and since half term she wasn't speaking to me at all. She'd been quite huffy when I rang her. I knew that I was the one who was in the wrong, which was why I was willing to say sorry, but I wasn't the one who'd broken our friendship by going and joining a gang, so I really didn't think she had any right to take offence. Not when I'd *apologised*. And to tell me I was disloyal, going out with Shay instead of with her, that was just, like, totally unfair. I wouldn't ever have hung out with Shay if Millie and me had still been friends.

"I've got to hang out with *someone*," I said. "If it weren't for Shay, I'd be on my own!"

"She's got you right where she wants you," said Millie. "She's only gotta call and you go running!"

We didn't actually have a bust-up, cos I just hate,

hate, HATE quarrelling with people, but the telephone call became very frosty, so that I could almost hear the ice crackling as we talked. And now she wasn't just not speaking to me, she wasn't even looking at me any more. Mum seemed to think it was all my fault. She said, "All this talk about gangs! We had gangs at my school. It didn't stop us being friends."

Mum didn't understand, and it was no use trying to explain. She had no idea what it was like, at Krapfilled High. She said, "You're so impressionable! You're far too easy to manipulate. That Shay has just mesmerised you."

Everyone seemed to have it in for Shay and I didn't know why. Karina sidled up to me one day, looking all sly and secretive and practically on the point of bursting with self-importance. She obviously had something she was dying to tell me, but I still remembered the early days, when she'd dripped poison in my ears, like about Mr Kirk beating his wife and Brett Thomas being on drugs, so I turned and walked away from her, hoping she'd get the message. She didn't, of course, or if she did, she ignored it. She really was one of those people it's impossible to snub.

"Hey!" She poked at me, from behind. I turned, rather irritably.

"What?"

"D'you want to hear something?"

I said, "Not particularly."

"I think you ought to," Karina said.

"Why?"

"Cos you ought to. It's something you ought to know. It's about your *friend*... Shay*anne*."

I should have told her to just shut up, or go away, but I'm not very good at being rude to people. Shay used to say that I was too polite. "It won't get you anywhere." It is true, I think, that there are times when you have to be a bit blunt. I did try! I said, "I don't listen to gossip," and marched off across the playground. But with Karina you would most likely have to bash her over the head with a brick before she took any notice.

"It's not gossip!"
She came scuttling
after me, like a big
spider, all eager to
spit venom, or
whatever spiders do.
"It's the honest truth!
Did you know—"
She lowered her
voice to a squeak.
"*Your friend* was
chucked out of both
the schools she used
to go to?"

Sniffily, pretending like mad, I said, "That's supposed to be news?"

Karina's face fell. "She told you?"

"Like you said, she's *my friend.*"

"I bet she didn't tell you why she was chucked out!"

I hesitated.

"She didn't, did she? D'you want me to?"

I tried to say no, but I wasn't quick enough. Karina just went rushing on.

"She *did* things. I can't tell you what things, but they were *bad* things. *Really* bad things. Now there aren't any more posh schools that will have her, which is why she's ended up here."

Karina looked at me, triumphantly. I said, "How do you know about it?"

"Cos I do. I know things."

It was true, Karina did know

things. She made it her business to pry into other people's affairs and "know things" about them. She'll probably grow up to be a professional blackmailer.

"I just thought I ought to warn you," she said, smugly. "I wouldn't want you getting into trouble, or anything. Cos that's what she does... she gets people into trouble. *You* think she's all lovely and sticking up for you, but what she's really doing is—"

"Stop it!" I said and I stamped my foot. I was so angry! "I don't want to hear. Shay is my *friend*."

I ran off as fast as I could. Karina's voice came shrieking after me: "You'll be sorry! You're making a big mistake!"

I tried to put out of my mind the things that Karina had told me. And the things that the girl in the shopping mall had said. *And* the uncomfortable feelings I'd had, once or twice. Shay was my friend and I owed her everything. I was doing my homework in the library, I was getting good marks – nearly all As! – and no one was bullying me or getting on my case. I wasn't going to listen to malicious gossip. Cos it *was* gossip, no matter what Karina chose to call it. It was gossip, and it was mean.

Sometimes, if Shay wasn't around, or even if she was, me and Varya would smile at each other and nod, just to be friendly. We still didn't actually talk, but I kept thinking of things that I might say to her, like "How did you get on with your maths homework last night?" or "Ugh! Yuck! Double PE this afternoon." Unfortunately, at the last minute, I'd either get stupidly tongue-tied or a teacher would appear and bellow at everyone to "Stop that confounded racket!" But I was determined that sooner or later I *would* try and start up a conversation.

It was like since meeting Shay I was getting something I'd never had before – confidence.

Like Julia and Jenice had a go at me one morning; they took advantage of Shay not being there.

"Look what the Geek is wearing!"

"That is just *so* cool!"

And then they both went off into these loud guffaws, like something out of a comic strip. If it had happened at the beginning of term I'd have been *mortified*. Well, I still was mortified to tell the truth, cos I knew I looked really stupid. My school shoes had got big holes in them and my trainers were falling to pieces, and Mum had said I'd better wear my wellies "just for today, as it's raining".

She'd promised to get me some new shoes for tomorrow, but tomorrow was too late. I wished I could have stayed at home! I couldn't, because Mum wouldn't let me, and suddenly I just felt so *angry*, I turned and shouted. I shouted, "SHUT UP, you

pair of blithering morons! You haven't got a brain between you!"

Julia said, "Ooh, blithering morons!" and Jenice gave a little titter, but after that, to my huge surprise, they left me in peace. I think they were just so taken aback that I'd dared to say anything. I was, too! But it did feel good.

One Saturday, a couple of weeks later, Shay suggested we go and have a look at the Elysian Fields, which was this huge out-of-town shopping centre that had just opened. It sounded like a really fun place, but I couldn't think how we'd get there. Shay said no problem, she'd get her dad to take us. "The Invisible Man", as she called him.

"We can get the bus back, there's one that goes all the way to my place. Then you could stay and have tea. Ask your mum!"

Mum wasn't all that keen, as I'd known she wouldn't be, but she said she supposed she'd have to agree to it if that was what I really wanted.

"But don't you let her go buying you things! And I

need you to be back no later than six. Is that understood?"

I solemnly promised, on both counts, and Shay said she'd call round with the Invisible Man and pick me up. Mum insisted on coming all the way downstairs, "just to make sure". When I said, "Make sure of what?" she muttered something about "Seeing you off". I knew that really she was just curious about Shay's dad. I was quite curious myself, and also a bit nervous, as I had no idea what he could be like.

He was sitting at the wheel of this big red car which Mum said afterwards was a Merc, meaning Mercedes.

 (I don't know anything about cars, I can't tell one from another.) He was creamy-skinned, like Shay ("Foreign extraction," said Mum), with glossy hair, very thick and black. He didn't look like a dad, he looked like a movie star. I was quite in awe of him, and I think Mum was, too, as she didn't say any of the things she'd said she was going to say, like "I've told Ruth she has to be home no later than six o'clock" and

175

"Would you please make sure to give her a lift back?" All she said was, "How do you do?" and "It's nice of you to drive them." I didn't say anything at all, but just slid into the back seat next to Shay.

We drove all the way to the shopping centre in total silence. Shay looked out of the window, her dad drove the car, and I chewed my fingernails, which is something I haven't done since I was quite tiny. It was really weird. (I don't mean me chewing my fingernails, I mean nobody speaking.) When we arrived, Shay and I got out, her dad said, "OK, you know how to get back," and that was that.

Like I said, weeeeeird!

"He's the quiet sort," said Shay. "He never says much. Not unless he's having a fight with the Vampire."

"They *fight*?" I said.

"Yeah. Don't yours?"

"They sometimes have words," I said, "but they don't actually fight."

Shay seemed to think that that was rather weird. She seemed to think that all parents fought.

"Let's forget about them," she said. "C'mon! Let's go up the escalator... we'll start at the top and work our way down."

Which is what we did. It was like being in an enchanted town! I reckon you could stay there all day and not get bored. It would take about *two weeks* to actually see everything.

"I need a snack," said Shay, after we'd been wandering in and out of shops and up and down escalators for a couple of hours. "Let's go in the Chocolate Shop and have a hot chocolate. It's all right, I'll pay! Your mum can't object to me just buying you something to drink."

In the Chocolate Shop they had real hand-made chocolates decorated with tiny rosebuds and violets. So sweet! I felt my mouth watering as I looked at them, but I didn't have any money to buy any and I couldn't have asked Shay. But she must have noticed me looking, cos after we'd finished our mugs of chocolate and left the shop she suddenly put her hand in her pocket and brought something out and said, "Close your eyes and open your mouth." And when I did, she popped a chocolate into it!

"*Oh.*" I munched, ecstatically.

"Good?" said Shay.

"Mm!"

"Have another."

She had a whole packet of them! I said, "How did you—"

"Just eat," said Shay. "Don't ask."

"But h—"

"I took them."

I said, "T-took them?"

"Took them! *Helped myself.*"

She meant that she'd stolen them. That she'd *shoplifted.* The bottom fell out of my stomach with a great clunk. I think my mouth must have fallen open, as Shay gave one of her cackles and said, "Are you shocked?"

I was – horribly. All of a sudden, I was thinking about my chain. And about the earrings. And the drawers full of make-up and jewellery.

"Honestly," said Shay, "you should see your face!" She pulled down the corners of her mouth and sucked in her cheeks. I felt like saying, "But it's *stealing.*" Only I couldn't, cos it sounded too goody-goody.

"Stop looking so disapproving! It's only a bit of fun. It's like a kind of game... seeing what you can get away with. I'm pretty good at it! I can get away with almost anything."

She was actually boasting about it. I couldn't believe it! Me and Millie had once gone sneaking into Woolworth's and nicked a handful of lollipops, but that was when we were about *six.* Well, eight, maybe. But we'd known that it was wrong and I think we'd both been secretly a bit ashamed of ourselves. At any rate, we'd never done it again. Shay had obviously been at it for ages.

"Oh, come on, Spice, lighten up! It's not like I'm mugging old ladies for their life savings. I'm not hurting anyone! I never lift anything valuable. Not like real diamonds or anything. Just stuff that takes my fancy. I do it for *fun*. Yeah?"

I couldn't speak. I just didn't know what to say.

"C'mon!" Shay linked her arm through mine. "Let's go and look in the music shop."

I didn't enjoy the music shop. I was on tenterhooks the whole time, in case something else took Shay's fancy and she put it in her pocket and marched out without paying.

All the really expensive stuff, like the DVDs and full-price CDs, were in those plastic cases that have to be removed before you can leave the shop or they'll set the alarm bells ringing. I relaxed a bit round those, cos I didn't think even

Shay would risk setting off alarm bells. But then we came to the bargain section, where they didn't bother with plastic cases, and I started to prickle and shake all over again as I watched Shay picking up bunches of CDs and shuffling them like cards.

"That's a fab one." She flashed a CD in front of me. I tried not to look, but she insisted. "Techno Freaks. They're brilliant! They're my favourite band."

"You'd better put it down," I said. "People are watching."

"So what?" said Shay, but to my great relief she put the CD back with the others and said, "OK! Let's go."

I'd thought once we were outside we'd be safe. Shay bought a couple of pop ices from a kiosk and we perched on a low wall, side by side, licking at them, and slowly I began to breathe a bit easier. But then Shay said, "Remember what you said the other day?"

I said, "What was that?"

"About wanting to give me something?" said Shay.

I felt my blood begin to grow chill.

"Y-yes," I said.

"Did you really mean it?"

I swallowed. "Y-yes," I said.

"OK, so if you really mean it... if you really, really mean it..."

I waited, in a kind of numb horror, for what she was going to say.

"I'd like you to get me that CD!"

I felt my face grow slowly crimson.

"Techno Freaks. The one I showed you. Yeah?"

"I haven't any money," I whispered.

"You don't need money! I told you, you just go in and take it... easy-peasy! I do it all the time."

I stood there, my heart hammering.

"What's the problem?" said Shay. "What are you waiting for?"

"I... I can't!" I said.

"Why can't you?"

"I just can't!"

"I thought you said you really, really wanted to get me something?"

I hung my head. My face was pulsating like a big hot tomato, but my hands were all clammy with sweat.

"Isn't that what you said?"

"Yes."

"So why won't you do it?"

"B-because—"

"Because what? Because you're scared?"

"Because it's stealing!" The words finally came blurting out of me.

"Oh! Shock horror! It's *stealing!*" Shay gave a loud squawk and threw up her hands. A woman passing by turned to stare, but Shay didn't seem to see. Or maybe she just didn't care? "These people make millions! How's it going to hurt them, just nicking one little CD? They probably wouldn't even notice it had gone!"

I couldn't think what to say to this. All I could think was that it was *wrong*.

"Do you want me to come with you," said Shay, "and hold your hand—"

"No! I'm not going to do it!"

"You mean you're not going to get me anything?"

"Not like that," I mumbled.

"So how are you going to do it, then?"

"I don't know! I'll... save up my pocket money, or something."

"Huh!"

"I will. I promise! I'll get you something."

"Not sure I want anything now."

"Oh, please!" I sprang after her, as she turned and began to walk away. "Shay, please!" I tugged at her sleeve. "I'll get you something really nice, something you'll really like. I'll get you the CD, the one you want—"

"It'll be too late by then. I'll have got it for myself, thank you very much. And *I* won't bother saving up for it! Or do you mean—" She suddenly whipped round, to face me. "Do you mean you're going to go and get it for me right now, after all?"

I felt myself start to shake. It would've been so much easier to say yes! To go back into the shop and slip the CD into my pocket and have Shay happy with me again.

"*Well?*"

"I can't!" My voice came out in a self-pitying bleat. Shay's face darkened.

"So what you said was just a load of rubbish, about really, really, *really* wanting to get me something."

"It wasn't! It wasn't rubbish!" I felt a flicker of anger, somewhere deep inside me. "I do really, really want to get you something, but not like this!"

"Like *what*?"

"Stealing. I don't care what you say! It's wrong to steal and I don't think you should to be doing it!"

"Why not, if I enjoy it?"

"Cos it's *beneath* you," I said.

She stopped. "What d'you mean, it's beneath me?"

"It's beneath you! It's a mindless blob sort of thing to do!" I hadn't know this was what I was going to say, but as soon as I'd said it I knew that it was right. "Mindless blobs go out and steal cos they can't think of anything else to do. You're not a mindless blob! You're oceans better than they are."

"That's what you think," muttered Shay.

"It's what I know. You can do anything you want! You don't need to go out and nick things. It's *unworthy*," I said.

"Wow! That's telling it like it is," said Shay. She was trying to make a joke of it, but I could see that I'd got through to her.

"I wish you wouldn't do it any more," I begged.

I trembled a bit as I said it, cos Shay could be quite a frightening sort of person. I really hated the thought of her being cross with me, maybe even stalking off and leaving me on my own, not wanting to be friends any more. But I knew I couldn't back down, not even if I was shaking like a leaf.

I think Shay was quite surprised; I don't think she'd ever imagined that I'd stand up to her. She looked at me for a moment through half-closed eyes, like she was trying to decide whether to be cold and cutting or just walk off; then suddenly she gave another of her cackles and said, "All right, then! Just for you."

I said, "F-for me?"

"Just for you... I'll stop doing it!"

I said, "You will?" I was stunned. I felt like I'd won the lottery! "You really mean it?"

"Watch my lips... what did I say? *Just-for-you.* I wouldn't stop doing it for anyone else, but I'm sick of you nagging at me!"

I said, "I wasn't nagging!"

"Course you were. Nag, nag, nag. Ooh, it's naughty! Ooh, it's stealing! And I still haven't got my CD."

"I'll get it for you, I'll save up for it!"

"Yeah, yeah, yeah." Shay waved a hand. "Don't bother, I don't really want it. I was just, like, testing you. Trying to see if you'd do it. It's probably just as well you didn't, you'd be bound to get caught."

"Yes, I would. I'd be shaking like a jelly."

"Dunno what I'm gonna do for kicks in future, mind you. Have to take up finger painting or something."

Greatly daring, I said, "You could always learn how to use a vacuum cleaner and tidy your room up."

"See what I mean?" said Shay. "Nag, nag, nag! I pity your husband if you ever get married... you'll drive him bonkers!"

For the first time, as we went back on the bus together, I felt that Shay and me were real proper friends, like I'd been with Millie. We were giggling together and sharing jokes, and I knew it was because I'd found the courage to stand  up to her. The girl who'd spoken to me that time in the shopping mall had said that Shay would "make me do things." I'd told her that I didn't do anything I didn't want to do and I hadn't! So I was quite proud of myself and felt that Shay respected me.

When we got off the bus she said, "Let's go and get some junk food for tea." I knew she was only getting junk food to annoy her mum, but I didn't say anything as I thought I'd probably said enough already. She'd promised to stop nicking stuff and that was the most important.

We went to a little corner shop that had one of those notices on the door: ONLY TWO SCHOOL CHILDREN AT A TIME. Shay said, "That's cos they steal things."

"Only if they're mindless blobs," I said.

"Yeah, right," said Shay.

We were in the shop, trying to decide what to buy, when I noticed that the old woman behind the counter was watching us. It made me uncomfortable, though I don't know why, since we weren't doing anything we shouldn't have been.

"How about this?" Shay picked up a packet of Starbursts. "And crisps! We gotta have crisps."

She was just reaching out for a bag of prawn cocktail when the old woman came over to us and snapped, "What are you two up to?" She must have had a *really* suspicious nature.

"Nothing," said Shay.

"Don't give me that! I saw you, trying to filch those crisps. I'm just about sick of you kids! You in particular." She snatched the bag from Shay and slapped it back on the shelf. "You've been in here before, haven't you?"

"So what if I have?" said Shay.

"I'll give you 'what if I have', my girl! And I'll have those back, as well!" She wrenched the Starbursts out of Shay's hand. "Nasty thieving brats, the pair of you!"

"Excuse me," I said. I was just so furious! What right had this horrible old woman to accuse us of stealing her rotten junky food? "We were going to *pay* for those!"

"Pull the other one," said the old woman. She gave me a shove. "And get out of my shop! You show your faces in here again and I'll have the law on you."

I screamed, "But we haven't *done* anything!"

It was Shay who grabbed me by the arm and pulled me away. I was really surprised that she hadn't answered back; I was the one practically beside myself with indignation.

"She hasn't any right to treat us like that! You can't go round accusing people of stealing when they haven't done anything. There's laws against doing that!"

I went on about it all the way back to Shay's place. It was so unfair – and especially to Shay. I couldn't understand why she wasn't more angry about it.

"I'd be *fuming*," I said.

"You *are* fuming," said Shay. "You're fuming enough for both of us." And then, in this very calm, laid-back sort of voice, she said that when she was really angry – "I mean really, *really*" – she didn't waste her energy shouting and banging around.

"I go away quietly and I plan things," she said. "That's what I'm gonna do now... I'm gonna go away all quietly and I'm gonna plan things. You'll see!"

Secret Writings of Shayanne Sugar

That old witch in the newspaper shop is gonna GET IT. She is gonna be WORKED OVER. She is gonna be DONE. I mean it!

She's got some cheek, accusing me of stealing. I might have done before, but I wasn't THIS TIME. I was actually gonna pay the old witch. Well, that's it. She's cooked her goose. Good and proper! Nobody, but NOBODY, messes with this baby and gets away with it. She has made one BIG MISTAKE.

Actually, I must have been mad. It was Spice's fault, she was the one talked me into it. "It's STEALING," she goes, all pathetic. So what do I do? I go and promise that I won't ever do it again, miss! I'm really sorry, miss! Please forgive me, miss! Dunno what came over me. I shoulda told her to get lost.

She's nothing to me! Why should I care what she thinks, stupid old Matchsticks. I don't care what ANYONE thinks. She's got some cheek, telling me I'm like a mindless blob. Never thought she'd have the guts. First one that ever has! Gotta give it to her. Still doesn't explain why I let her get to me. Must be going soft inna head. TEMPORARY INSANITY. Yeah, and see where it's got me. Some old witch has the nerve to actually threaten me with the police!!!! ME. When I wasn't DOING anything.

Well, that's it. She's asked for it. She is gonna be HUNG OUT TO DRY.

And Spice is gonna help me do it...

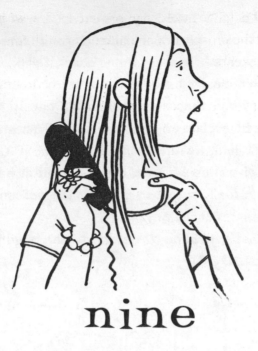

nine

I was so excited when Shay rang me, Sunday morning, to say why didn't I stay over at her place next weekend. It was Lisa who answered the phone. She yelled, "Ruth-it's-for-you-it's-that-girl!" The way she said it, *that girl*, it was like Shay had crawled out of a garbage dump. She'd picked it up from Mum. She knew Mum didn't approve, so now she didn't, either. It was totally mindless and it made me cross, especially since me and Shay had become real, true and proper friends. What right had my snotty little sister to be so high and mighty? I'd have ticked her off except I was just so thrilled at the prospect of actually being with Shay for a whole weekend.

"I'll even clear a bit of space in my bedroom," she said. "Just for you... cos we're friends!"

I immediately rushed off to ask Mum. To begin with my heart was in my mouth as I thought she was going to say no. I just couldn't bear it if she said no! It was Dad who came to my rescue. He said, "Oh, come on, Lynn! What harm can it do?"

"There's just something about that girl," said Mum. "I don't trust her."

Needless to say, Lisa was standing there with her ears going tick tock. I knew she was taking it all in and that later on she'd repeat it to me, parrot fashion.

"That girl... we don't trust her!"

Without having the faintest idea *why*. I don't think Mum ought to say these sort of things in front of Lisa; she's too young and stupid.

Anyway, Dad stuck up for me and in the end Mum gave in. She said all right, I could go, even though she wasn't happy about it.

"But since she seems to be the only friend you have—"

"She's my *best* friend," I said.

"Well, just be careful," said Mum.

What did she mean, *be careful*? What was there to be careful about? It didn't make any sense.

"Don't let her lead you astray."

Mum thought I was such a pushover I'd do whatever Shay asked me to do. Little did she know that I was the one who'd got Shay to turn over a new leaf! I'd stood up to her. I wasn't anywhere near as weak and feeble as Mum made me out to be.

On Saturday afternoon I met Shay in the shopping centre and we went into Marks & Spencer and bought stuff for tea. Mum never goes into Marks & Spencer, she says we can't afford it, but Shay said I had to have the best, "Cos you're my friend... and look, I'm paying for it! See? It'd be just as easy not to, but I'm doing it for you... cos you're my *friend*."

She'd cleared a bit of space in her bedroom, too, just like she'd promised. It wasn't very much space, and I thought that most probably all she'd done was just kick stuff out of the way, but at least there was a sort of path across the middle of the carpet.

Shay said that we'd have to sleep in the same bed, "Cos I haven't got a sleeping bag and you don't want to go in the spare room all by yourself, do you?"

I agreed that I didn't. The whole point of a sleepover is to be together, so you can lie there all nice and cosy in the darkness, giggling and swapping secrets. I said this to Shay and she said, "Well, this is it. This is what I said to the Vampire. *She* thought you were going to sleep in the spare room."

"Where is she?" I said. "Is she…" I giggled, "…in her coffin?"

"Nah, she's gone off for the weekend. Took her coffin with her. *He's* here. The Invisible Man. D'you wanna see him?"

I giggled again. I was getting used to the way Shay referred to her mum and dad.

"Don't see how I can, if he's invisible!"

"Yeah, good point," said Shay. "Let's have some music."

We spent the afternoon listening to various CDs that Shay dug out from the mounds of books and clothes and magazines that littered the floor, then went downstairs to eat our Marks & Spencer's tea. Shay's dad looked round the door as we were in the middle of it and said, "Oh, hallo… um… Rosie?"

"Ruth," snapped Shay.

"Ruth. Hallo!"

I said hallo back, turning a bit pink. I don't know why I found it so embarrassing, being in the same room as Shay's dad, but he just looked so totally un-dadlike. If she'd have said he was a movie star or a famous tennis player, I wouldn't have been surprised.

"I'm off out," he said. "I'll be back about elevenish. You OK here by yourselves?"

"What if I said no?" said Shay.

Her dad blinked. "Well, I guess I'd have to have a rethink. But there are two of you, so you won't be lonely. Just don't answer the door. Usual precautions. Oh, and you've got my mobile number if you need it. OK?"

Shay's dad went breezing out, leaving us on our own.

"What would happen if I wasn't here?" I asked.

"What d'you mean?" said Shay.

"Like... would he still go out and leave you?"

"They always go out on a Saturday. Both of 'em."

"Doesn't it bother you?"

"Nah! Why should it?"

"It'd bother me," I said.

"I'm used to it. They've always done it. Even when I was tiny. They never really wanted a kid in the first place."

"How d'you know?" I said.

"Cos she told me."

"Your mum? She *told* you?"

"Yeah. She said I was lucky she didn't have an abortion and get rid of me."

I could feel my eyes growing huge as saucepan lids. I couldn't believe what I was hearing!

"Welcome to the real world," said Shay. "Let's go and watch a video."

We watched videos and played computer games all evening, until suddenly, at about eleven o'clock, Shay jumped up and said, "Right! Time to go out."

I said, "*Out?* But it's dark!"

"Yeah? So what? I often go out in the dark. C'mon! There's something we gotta do."

"What?" I hurried anxiously after her as she went out into the hall. "What have we got to do?"

"Tell you when we get there. Here!" She flung my coat at me. "I just gotta fetch something. Won't be a sec."

She went down the stairs into the kitchen and came back up with a plastic carrier bag.

"OK! Let's go."

I was quite nervous, being out so late. I'm *never* out that late, not even with Mum. I mean, we just never really go anywhere; we can't, because of Dad. I kept telling myself that Shay did it all the time, so it had to be all right. But I knew that it wasn't. Not really. I knew that Mum would be horrified if she ever found out.

"W-where exactly are we going?" I said.

"Just into town a bit. Back to the shop."

I said, "What shop?"

"Shop where the old witch accused us of stealing."

I felt a row of prickles go tingling down my spine. "W-won't they be closed?" I said.

"Hope so," said Shay. She cackled. "Better had be!"

"So w-what are we going there for?"

"Gonna teach her a lesson is what we're going there for. It's all right! You don't have to *do* anything. Just be there."

I desperately didn't want to be there. Whatever it was that Shay was planning to do, I didn't want any part of it! But I was too scared to turn round and walk away, all by myself. For one thing, I wasn't sure I could remember how to get back to Shay's place, and even if I did get back, I didn't have a key.

Reluctantly, I trailed after Shay. The shop was on a corner. The shutter was pulled down over the door, and wire mesh screens were over the windows. All the other shops nearby were closed, and the street was empty.

Shay said, "Good! You stay here and keep a look-out. I'm going down the side. If you see anyone coming, you gotta let me know. OK?"

I nodded, miserably.

"Look, we're *friends*," said Shay. "It's what friends do... they watch out for each other. It's all I'm asking... just watch out for me."

She made it sound like I'd be really letting her down if I didn't do it.

"Anyone comes, you tell me. Yeah?"

I said, "Yes, but wh—"

"Don't ask! It's best you don't know. You're already an accomplice, of course—" I felt my legs begin to wobble. "But you can always say you didn't know what was going on. If anyone asks, that is. But no one's going to ask. Are they? Cos you're gonna keep a look-out! Here, just hang on to the bag."

Shay took something from it, then thrust it at me and disappeared down the side, leaving me to stand shivering on the corner. It wasn't really cold, but my kneecaps were bounding and my teeth kept clattering. I think it was because I was just so terrified.

Cars passed, but no people. A police car came down the road and slowed up as it approached. I did my best to look brave and confident, like I was just standing there waiting for someone, and to my relief it drove on. I was so busy watching it, making sure it didn't turn round and come back, that I didn't notice a street door opening at the side of the shop. A man came out, followed by a woman. I nearly died of fright! It was the old witch woman that had accused us of stealing. She didn't look quite as ancient as she had in the shop – and the man didn't look ancient at all. He was big and burly, like a rugby player. I gave a panic-stricken squeak and dashed off round the side.

"Someone's coming!"

Shay immediately stopped whatever it was she was doing and ran for it. I made to run after her, but the rugby player had me in his grasp.

"What the—"

I squealed and wriggled, but he just held on even tighter.

"Is this you?" He gestured furiously at the side wall of the shop. Someone had spray-canned all over it – **DEATH AND DESTRUCTION** – in big letters, plus lots of really creepy drawings of skulls and crossbones and hangman's nooses.

The old witch woman had appeared.

"You're one of those kids," she said. "I recognise you! What's in that bag? What have you got in there?" She snatched it away from me. "I thought as much!"

Triumphantly, she brought out a can of spray paint. Black, the same as the stuff on the wall. "Caught you red-handed, my pretty! Just as well my son's a fast mover... thought you'd get away with it, didn't you?"

"I don't reckon she was the one actually did it." The man still had a grip on me; his fingers were really biting into my arm. "I reckon she was just the lookout."

"No!" I shook my head. "It was just me!"

I don't know why I said that, except that Shay had obviously managed to escape and I didn't want to get her into trouble. After all, the old witch *had* falsely accused her.

"I did it by myself," I said.

They obviously weren't sure whether to believe me. The man said, "Are you telling the truth?"

"Yes! It was me on my own!"

A new voice broke in. "Don't believe her! She wouldn't dare!"

I spun round. It was Shay! She'd come back! The man immediately pounced on her.

"I knew it! I knew there was another of 'em!"

"You don't have to break my arm," said Shay.

"I'll do more than break your arm, you little vandal,

I'll— *Ow!*" He jumped back, with a curse, as Shay kicked out. "You little brat!"

"I told you, you don't have to break my arm! I'm not going anywhere. Wouldn't have come back if I was planning on going anywhere."

I don't know why she had come back. She could have got away quite easily – no one need ever have known. I wouldn't have told on her, no matter what they did to me. I really wouldn't! I was her friend. Friends don't betray each other. But oh, at the time, I was just so relieved!

The old woman's son wanted to turn us over to the police, but the old witch woman said no.

"Not that they don't deserve it, but I know this one." She pointed at Shay. "I know her mum and dad – they come into the shop quite often. Nice, respectable people. I think we'll go and see what they have to say."

"They're not there," said Shay.

"Well, let's just go and check that out, shall we?"

"You're wasting your time. She's away and he's out with his girlfriend."

But he wasn't. When we got back to Shay's place, her dad was there and already had a face like thunder.

"Where in God's name have you been? What do you think you're doing, going out at this time of night?"

"Vandalising my property," said the witch woman, "that's what they're doing!"

Shay's dad was horribly angry. I mean, like, really,

really angry. Cold and cutting, and his lips going into a thin line.

"What is the *matter* with you?" He took Shay by the shoulders and shook her. "Do you do this just to spite us? Don't you have everything you could possibly want? Everything that money could buy? Dear God! How many more times?"

Shay just stood, saying nothing. Needless to say, I said nothing, either. I couldn't have, even if anyone had wanted me to. My teeth were clattering and I felt like I was about to be sick.

Shay's dad had started to shout. "Are you some kind of delinquent? Do we have to have you put away?"

"Yeah, get someone else to deal with the mess," said Shay.

Honestly! I don't know how she dared. Her dad drew a deep breath, like he was trying very hard to control himself, and turned to the witch woman. Stiffly, he told her that of course he'd see that all the graffiti was removed from her wall and he thanked her for not going to the police. She said, "Well, my son wanted me to, but seeing as I know you... I thought maybe you'd rather deal with it yourself." Shay's dad said grimly that he most certainly would.

"You can rest assured of that." And he gave Shay this really black look as he said it, so I knew she was going to be in big, BIG trouble. And so was I. Being an accomplice is just as bad as actually committing the crime; we'd both have been locked up if the old woman's son had had his way. I would've died if that had happened! I'd have been so ashamed. I was ashamed enough as it was, cos I'd never done anything like that in my life before. I'd never done anything criminal at all, except for stealing the lollipops in

Woolworths, but that was when I was tiny. And that was just, like, being naughty. Spraying skulls and crossbones on the side of someone's wall, that was *serious*.

Shay's dad told us to "Wait in there, both of you, while I get something to compensate this good woman," and he pushed us quite roughly into the front room and shut the door. He was *angry*.

I whispered, "What's going to happen?"

Shay shrugged her shoulders. "Dunno. Who cares? You don't have to be involved! It's not like you did anything."

"But I was an ac-complice," I said.

"Yeah, but you didn't know what was going on. I'll tell 'em! Don't worry."

"But w-what about you?"

"Doesn't matter about me. I can look after myself."

"You shouldn't have come back!" I said.

"Had to," said Shay. "Couldn't leave you on your own." And then she said such a curious thing, she said, "Wouldn't have done it for anyone else. Just for you. cos you're different."

I shall always remember Shay saying that. I wished I'd asked her how! "*How* am I different?" At the time I was too worried sick even to think of it. Shay honestly didn't seem in the least bit bothered, but I was petrified. I've never been so scared in all my life! Shay couldn't understand it. She said, "Oh, come on, Spice, you didn't *do* anything. What are you scared of?"

What I was scared of was what Mum and Dad were going to say. Shay still couldn't understand it. She said, "Don't see why they should say anything. Don't have to know, do they? Who's gonna tell 'em? Not me!"

"But I c-can't let you take all the blame," I said.

"Why not?"

"Well, because... because we're friends!"

"It's because we're *friends*," said Shay, "that I'm gonna keep you out of it. It's what friends do... they look after each other. Anyway, it's not gonna help me any, you getting into trouble. Prob'ly just make it worse."

So then I thought that perhaps she was right, and Mum and Dad need never know, and this cheered me up a bit and made me feel stronger, until Shay's dad reappeared and snapped, "Right, young woman!" He meant *me*. "Let's get you back home."

"She's staying over," said Shay.

"Not any more, she's not. She's going home, and you and I are going to have a serious talk. Come along! The pair of you."

"Don't see why I have to go," said Shay.

"You'll do as you're told! Get a move on."

"I don't want to," said Shay. "I want to stay where I am."

"You really think I'd be fool enough to go off and

leave you here to get up to heaven knows what?"

"Yeah, why not?" said Shay. "It's what you usually do."

"What I may have done in the past, my girl, and what's going to happen in the future, are two entirely different things. Leave you here and risk getting back to find the place burnt to a cinder? No, thank you! I know what you're capable of. Now, shift yourself!"

We drove home in total silence. Shay was in such a sulk she didn't even say goodbye to me. Her dad asked me if I wanted him to see me to my front door, but although I was scared of using the lift at that time of night, I was even more scared of him coming with me and talking to Mum, so I said that I'd be all right. He said, "You sure?" and I said "Yes!" and shot out of the car before he could change his mind.

It was nearly midnight when I rang the bell. Mum and Dad would be in bed; they might even be asleep. But I couldn't stand outside all night! I rang and rang, and then called out through the letter box, "Mum, it's me!" If I hadn't called she might never have come, cos everyone's, like, really nervous once it gets dark. A lot of mugging and stuff goes on. Even though I'd called out, Mum still only opened the door a tiny crack and kept the chain on. And then she saw that it really was me, and she went *"Ruth?"* and took the chain off and quickly pulled me inside. "What are you doing here? I thought you were staying over! You haven't quarrelled, have you? They didn't let you come home by yourself?"

"N-no," I said. "Sh-shay's dad brought me."

"But why? Ruth! *Why*? What's going on?"

That was when I burst into tears and told her the whole story.

"I knew it," said Mum. "I knew something like this would happen. Didn't I say all along? There was just something about that girl?"

"It wasn't her fault," I sobbed. "The woman accused her!"

"That's no excuse. And now look what you've done! You've got your dad up."

Dad had appeared at the end of the passage. "What is it?" he said. "What's all the rumpus?"

"It's all right," said Mum. "It's just Ruth come back. Get to bed, now," she told me. "We'll talk about it in the morning."

"Not in front of Lisa!" I begged.

Mum agreed, not in front of Lisa. It was a bit of a comfort, but only a little bit.

Next morning, Mum shut the girls and Sammy away and we had our talk. Me and Mum and Dad. Mum said that she obviously couldn't stop me speaking to Shay at school, "But I don't want you seeing her out of school any more. I don't even want you ringing her. I don't want you having anything to do with her! Do you understand?"

I nodded, miserably.

"I want you to promise me," said Mum. "On your honour!"

I had to promise; what else could I do?

"It's for your own good," said Mum. "A girl like that, she's a really bad influence. It bothers me that you'll still be with her at school."

Mum needn't have worried. Shay didn't come into school on Monday; she wasn't there all the rest of the week. Jenice Berry, who bunked off whenever she felt like it, said that she'd seen her hanging about in the shopping centre. And then, the following week, she came up to me and said, "Well, have I got news for *you*! Your friend Shayanne Sugar's gone and got herself nicked." Karina, who was there at my elbow, immediately squealed, "What for? What was she doing?"

"*Stealing*." Jenice said it with relish; you could tell she was really enjoying herself. "In HMV. I was in there and I saw her being taken away. I don't reckon she'll be back!"

She never was. That night when I was brought home in disgrace was the last time I ever saw her. I did so long to know what had happened to her! I begged Mum to let me ring her, but Mum stood firm.

"It's best you just forget her," she said.

But how could I? I'll never forget Shay, as long as I live! When I'm grown up, and have passed all my exams, and have become a doctor working in a hospital – cos that *is* what I'm going to do – it will be all thanks to Shay. If it hadn't been for her, I'd just have given up.

I've puzzled and puzzled why she ever bothered with me. I can still remember, right at the beginning, when she told me that maths was not her favourite subject, and I said how it wasn't mine, either, and she said, "Well, that's one thing we have in common." But we didn't really have *anything* in common. Not really. Not even maths! Shay was good at maths. She was good at lots of things, but it was like she had this auto-destruct button inside her which she just couldn't resist pressing. If ever it looked like she might be going to do something people would approve of, where they might say "Well done!" or "Good work!" she immediately had to go and press the button – **BOOM!** – so it all blew up in her face. Like if one week she got an A for her homework it seemed the following week she'd just have to get a D, or even an E. Or even, sometimes, no mark at all, when she'd filled the pages with her big angry scribble.

Shay could have got As practically all the time if she'd wanted, and I could never understand why she didn't. I think now that maybe she didn't understand, either, or that she did understand but there just wasn't anything she could do about it, and that's why she got so cross whenever I tried asking her. And cross when I let people like Julia get to me. It was like I had to use *my* brain to make up for her not using hers. It wasn't that she didn't *want* to use hers; she just couldn't let herself. Maybe it was her way of getting back at her mum and dad for the way they treated her. That's the only thing I can think of.

I tried explaining all this to Mum. I so desperately

didn't want Mum to think badly of Shay! I told her about Shay's mum and dad, and how they used to go away and leave her on her own, sometimes for days and days. Mum was quite shocked. "I didn't know that," she said. "That's terrible!" And then she suddenly hugged me, which is something that Mum doesn't do all that often; I mean, she just doesn't have the time. She said, "Oh, Ruth, I know things haven't been easy for you, but we'll try to make them better. We'll get things sorted! It's not fair, putting all the burden on you, just because you're the oldest."

I don't know why Mum felt she had to apologise. It's not her fault if Dad's sick and can't work and I was born first. I told her this. I said, "I'd rather have you as a mum than have a mum like Shay's!" I think that made her happy cos she kissed me – which is something else she doesn't have time to do, usually – and said, "You're a good girl! I'll make it up to you. I promise! I won't let the others interfere when you want to do your homework."

She doesn't, either! She shoos them away and tells them to "*Be quiet.* Your sister's working." Ooh, it makes such a difference! They creep off as meek as mice and it means that I'm able to *concentrate.* I still go to the library sometimes, though. I've joined a homework club, which is fun, as you get to meet lots of people. The kids at school, they've mostly stopped bothering me. Just now and again the two Js try it on, like it's a sort of habit they can't break, but nobody takes much notice of them any more. Including me! The other day that horrible boy, Brett Thomas, told them to belt up. He shouted, "Knock it off, I'm sick of it!" Maybe he's not quite as horrible as I thought he was.

Actually, nothing is
– as horrible, I mean.
Things are getting
better all the time! I had
a long talk with Varya,
the day we went back
for the autumn term.
I've discovered that she's really nice. Her English has
hugely improved, it's almost as good as mine! This is
because I'm helping her. We hang out together and I give
her lessons. Mum and Dad have put in for a new flat from
the Council, one with more rooms, and if we get it, which
Mum seems to think we might, I could have a room all to
myself! Hooray! Varya could then come and stay with
me and that would be neat, as I've already been to stay
with her twice. I'd really love to invite her back.

One morning, about a
week ago, a card came
through the letter-box
with my name on it. It
was from Shay! Mum
didn't try keeping it
from me. She said,
"Here, it's for you. I
haven't read it." It didn't
really say very much; just a few words, in Shay's
big bold writing. But at least she'd written!

Wotcher, Spice! They've got me banged
up, boo hoo! Think I'm too dangerous to be
let out with all you law-abiding lot. Hope
you're working hard and giving the blobs
what for. YOU'D BETTER BE. See ya! – S.

I asked Mum if I could write back to her. There
wasn't any address, but I thought that if I sent a letter to
her home, her mum and dad might forward it. Mum was
reluctant at first, but then she relented, and so that's
what I'm going to do. She might not reply, but at any
rate I'll have tried. Even Mum has softened. She said
the other day, "That poor girl! She never stood a
chance."

I thought to myself that without Shay I'd never have
stood a chance. I know now that I can look after myself.
I can survive! I'm not a scaredy cat any longer. If
someone like *Joolyer* gives me any trouble – well!
She'd better just watch out, cos she'll get trouble back.
You have to be prepared to stand up for yourself; Shay
taught me that.

I shall never stop thinking about Shay, and
wondering how she is. I know it's true that she used
people, and that I let myself be bullied by her. But I did
speak up in the end! I didn't go stealing when she
wanted me to. And even though she tried to trick me,
that last night, when she sprayed the graffiti, she did

come back for me. She didn't have to; she could just have run away. I wouldn't ever have told on her! The thumbscrew and the rack wouldn't have got her name out of me. She only came back because in spite of everything, she was my friend.

She *was* my friend – I don't care what anyone says!

Is Anybody There?

Last year, I did this really dumb thing.
I got into a car with somebody
I didn't know...

If mum had been an ordinary mum, she might have
got the truth out of me. But she's not an ordinary mum,
she's a clairvoyant, and she's always careful not to pry.
I didn't even tell Dee and Chloe, my two best friends.
And now I'm not the only one in trouble...

0-00-716136-0

Check out Jean Ure's website: www.jeanure.com
www.harpercollinschildrensbooks.co.uk

www.jeanure.com

Secret Meeting

"I'm your fairy godmother!" Annie sprang
off the bed and did a little twirl.
"I'm the one that makes your
dreams come true!"

Annie's arranged the coolest birthday present for her
best friend, Megan. She's surfed the Net, made the contacts,
and it's all sorted! Now all they need to do is to escape from
Annie's bossy older sister. Cos a secret meeting wouldn't
be the same if it wasn't, well, secret…

0-00-715620-0

Check out Jean Ure's website: www.jeanure.com
www.harpercollinschildrensbooks.co.uk

Passion Flower

Of course, Mum shouldn't have
thrown the frying pan at Dad.
The day after she threw it,
Dad left home...

Stand back! Family Disaster Area! After the Frying Pan
Incident, it looks like me and the Afterthought are going
to be part of a single-parent family. Personally, I'm on Mum's
side but the Afterthought is Dad's number one fan. Typical.
Still, Dad's got us for the whole summer and things are
looking promising: no rules, no hassle, no worries.
But things never turn out the way you think.

0 00 715619 7

Check out Jean Ure's website: www.jeanure.com
www.harpercollinschildrensbooks.co.uk

Pumpkin Pie

This is the story of a drop-dead gorgeous girl
called Pumpkin, who has long blonde hair
and a figure to die for.
I wish!

It's my sister Petal who has the figure to die for. I'm the
one in the middle... the plump one. The other's the boy
genius, my brainy little brother, Pip. Then there's Mum,
who's a high flier and hardly ever around; and Dad, who's
a chef. Dad really loves to see me eat! I used to love to
eat, too. I never wanted food to turn into my enemy,
but when Dad started calling me *Plumpkin* I didn't
feel I had any choice...

0 00 714392 3